THE GHOST OF *GREYSON HALL*

A British Agent Novella

MK McCLINTOCK

TRAPPERS PEAK PUBLISHING

Published by Trappers Peak Publishing in the United States of America. www.mkmcclintock.com

The Ghost of Greyson Hall; novella/MK McClintock

ISBN: 978-1737758808

Paperback Edition

Cover Design by MK McClintock

For all those who believe in love so strong and pure,
it can reach across the centuries into forever.

PROLOGUE

In the year of 1782, among the snow-dusted hills of Northumberland, Lady Grace Canterbury of Greyson Hall disappeared.

Rumors abounded. She ran away with her Highland lover, leaving her husband and son behind. Others speculated on her declining health, claiming she'd gone away to die in solitude when the fever and pain overcame her body and mind. Those who knew her never believed the gossip and resolved through the years that ruffians kidnapped her at the command of her jealous husband.

No one ever learned the truth. Lady Canterbury vanished.

She'd left behind an infant son, who had barely found comfort in his mother's arms. A fair-haired and handsome boy who resembled his mother in coloring, including the eyes, ice blue and startling cold if it had not been for the spray of thick, black lashes.

Before the birth, Lord Spencer Canterbury had shared with her how he longed for a fair-haired daughter who looked like her mother. However, when their son made his first appearance, she saw her husband's joy in knowing it was a strong and healthy boy who would one day inherit the title and become master of their vast estate.

How does such a lady vanish without leaving a remnant of evidence?

For more than a century, the truth remained a mystery. Lady Canterbury became a faded memory, a story to entertain and bewilder at celebrations and gatherings. For generations, speculation continued. Descendants of the family attempted to unravel the mystery of the eighteenth-century puzzle, alas to no avail. Few took the matter seriously —after all, it was long before their time—and the image of a graceful beauty with hair as pale as the risen moon and eyes the color of waves on the sea faded into history.

CHAPTER 1

Greyson Hall, Northumberland
December 20, 1892

Devon walked the bedecked halls of the impressive estate he inherited over a year ago from an uncle he barely knew. Far removed from society's prying eyes and the adventure he craved during his years in service to the crown, Greyson Hall now represented family, future, and stability.

He no longer viewed the house as massive stones waiting to crumble and requiring constant upkeep. Greyson Hall offered shelter from the snow and rain, warmth from the cold, and employment to several who might otherwise be without. If someone had asked him a year ago where he lived, he would have said a well-appointed townhouse in London or one of the safe houses he often frequented when on a mission. London had merely been a place he rested his head between assignments and where his belongings gathered dust.

Then he met Anne. She became the home of his heart, even as the magnificent stone mansion became the home of their dreams.

With December upon them, and this, their first Christmas as a family and their first Christmas at Greyson Hall, he no longer existed—he lived and loved and thanked his God every night and every morning for the precious gift of his wife.

Anne's smile radiated a warmth and enduring love Devon treasured whenever in her presence. She had drawn him up from the dark ashes of a life and career he thought he wanted into a peaceful existence Devon never imagined he would be lucky enough to possess.

Anne's arms circled him from behind, her cheek pressed against his back. "Will the weather delay them, do you think?"

Devon held her close and gazed out the floor-to-ceiling window in his study. Gusts from the south blew fresh snow across the vast landscape, and swaying trees danced back and forth in time with the wind. "Tristan and Christopher may stop if they find shelter, but by my calculations, they will be too far along in their respective journeys now to turn back. Safer for them to continue."

"Seeing them all again after so many months will be wonderful. I checked the guest rooms, and the maids did wonderful work readying everything. And, we closed the last bedroom in the right wing, the old nursery. A dreadful draft has moved in, and the maids could not locate the source, so we transformed another room, closer to their suite, into a new nursery for Alaina's sons and their nanny. I never understood why a nursery must be so far away. I'm telling you now, Devon, our children will be close at hand."

"And how many little ones did you . . ." Devon's thoughts shifted to her earlier comment. "What draft?" He turned so she faced him, and his hands settled at her waist. "I examined every room in this manor before the weather turned."

"It is an immense house, my love." Anne brushed a kiss on his lips. "There is bound to be an occasional draft."

Devon pressed a kiss to his wife's brow and smiled. "Where did you say? Last bedroom in the east wing. The old nursery, yes. I will see to it."

Anne whirled around when he walked away. "You cannot mean to do that now. Our guests will arrive soon."

Devon waved a hand in the air. "Won't take long." The plush carpets muffled Devon's footfalls as he walked through the parlor to the study and into the hall. The grand entrance hall could easily double as a ballroom—if Devon was the sort to host a ball—and the staircase could manage a team of horses and the width of a coach.

He bounded up the stairs and stopped long enough to peer over the polished railing. From this vantage, he enjoyed a view of the smaller of Anne's two pine trees, dressed with yards of ribbon, garlands of dried fruit, and wax tapers that would be lit on Christmas Eve.

To his blessed relief, Anne possessed no desire to host balls, either, or anything more than the occasional dinner. He'd grown accustomed to a quieter life in Northumberland, far from the chaos, death, and disappointments he, Tristan, and Charles had suffered on numerous occasions while in service to Her Majesty.

A duke, an earl, and a mere mister, each willing to sacrifice the dream of a family to serve their king and country. The three men had become allies by necessity, friends through trust, and brothers of the heart through loyalty and devotion. Of course, not one of them had anticipated meeting the brave and remarkable women whose love promised a life apart from cold beds, scar-ridden bodies, and more secrets than any one person should have to keep.

Love, unwavering and eternal, was the legacy they could now pass onto their sons and daughters. Devon planned to revive the talk of little ones with Anne at the first opportunity. For now, he continued down the landing to the east wing, where his younger brothers, Derek and Zachary, occupied rooms when they were in residence. They still served as trusted agents to the crown and rarely spent more than a week a month at Greyson Hall.

Devon stopped at the first bedroom, the original nursery, and opened the door. The draft Anne mentioned coursed over his face and bare hands before he even entered. "Of course, there's a draft without heat." He found the vent, knelt, and held a hand over it. The servants kept the coal furnace fueled most of the day, and though not an ideal system, it warmed the impressive house to a reasonable degree of comfort. Natural convection was indeed pushing some of the heat into the room.

He stood and examined each window. Each one was secure, and the cold glass panes did not explain the draft still flowing around him. Devon examined the padded bench at a corner dressing table, determined it would hold his weight, and moved it next to the wardrobe. He reached a hand along the edges of the ceiling, to no avail.

"You must find country life far more tedious than I do if you've resorted to dusting corners for cobwebs. It has only been three months since your retirement."

Without looking at his friend, Devon stepped off the stool and asked Charles, "Do you feel a draft?"

"All these country houses have drafts. It's a requirement. The attics at Blackwood Crossing have several, and no matter who looks at it or how often we have crevices filled or the roof repaired, the drafts remain."

"You don't feel it?"

"Sure. A fire should do away with it."

"I'm not certain." Devon finally turned to Charles and smiled. "I'll deal with it later. It's good to see you, old friend." When they exited the bedroom, Devon closed the door, immediately dissipating the draft. "How is your beautiful wife?"

"Radiant as always, though tired."

Devon stopped on the top landing. "Is everything all right? The baby?"

"Yes, they are both well. A few irritations at Rhona's property in Scotland. Too many farmers in need of work and not enough landed gentry to support them. The former manager refused to hire anyone else."

"Former?"

Charles nodded. "Employed by Rhona's father and not at all loyal to her. Irritations, all managed for now. As soon as we found a new manager, we came immediately here. Roz doesn't need the stress in her condition, but it happens Greyson Hall is a perfect resting point before we return to the Crossing after the holidays."

They took the steps down slowly, content to share the latest news in quiet before they reached their wives. When they entered the parlor, Anne and Rhona were engrossed with a gilded cameo brooch presently resting in Anne's palm. Devon first crossed the room to Charles's wife and bent over to kiss her cheek lightly.

"You are well?"

Rhona's stormy blue eyes gazed up at Devon warmly. "Now that we are out of the weather and the jarring coach. One would think that the engineering marvels of our day could design a coach to glide over ruts. Why do we all live so far away from the nearest railways?"

"You detest most forms of civilization," Devon teased.

"Come to think of it, Zachary is the only one with a taste for city life, though he prefers Edinburgh to London. I will accept a jarring coach ride if those engineering marvels resolve London's soot and stench problem."

"Speaking of your brothers, Devon, how are they?" Charles asked. "Are Zachary and Derek still working together?"

"Not this time. Zachary is in Dublin, and Derek was called to Yorkshire."

Rhona leaned into the hand Charles rested on her shoulder. "They will be here for Christmas, won't they?"

Devon nodded. "They have promised not to disappoint." He peered over his wife at the brooch. "Where did that come from?"

Anne smoothed a finger over the elegant gold leaf etched into silver on the back of the brooch. "Elsie, the new maid, found it beneath the cupboard in Zachary's room when she took it upon herself to dust underneath the furniture. The mystery is how it came to be there."

Since neither of his brothers entertained female companions at Greyson Hall, Devon dismissed the possibility of it belonging to someone of Zachary's acquaintance. "It's familiar. And Elsie deserves a raise."

"I'll see to it. As for the brooch, it appears to have a hinge, but I've never seen such a piece of jewelry." Anne tried the clasp, stubborn in its resistance to release its hold. "It won't open." She handed it to Devon. "And it is a stunning piece."

Devon examined the brooch, searching his memory for where he'd seen the portrait. The etching on the back also tugged at his mind. "Tristan has made a study of various marks since his retirement, so while we await the Sheffield contingent . . . ah, the wait sounds to be over."

Charles and Devon walked out into the blustering cold to

greet the Sheffield coach while Anne and Rhona waited inside near the door with a view through a window. Devon reached the coach door immediately after the footman opened it to his friends. "Another hour and you would have had to stop at an inn."

Tristan alighted, then turned to help first his son, Christian, then accepted the bundled form of their younger son, Ambrose, from Alaina's arms.

"Hand him over, Tristan, and see to your wife." Devon gently lifted Ambrose into his arms and smiled at the cherub face peering at him. "Lucky for you, old man, your sons are the image of your wife."

Alaina's laughter warmed the frigid air as Tristan half-lifted her from the coach. "I recall you spoke similar words when Christian was born."

Charles kissed Alaina's cheeks and enjoyed his first look at Ambrose Sheffield. "Devon is right."

"I'm always right." Devon leaned over, careful of the boy, and kissed Alaina's proffered cheek. "I'll hand him back now, but I warn you, Anne will want to steal him the moment you cross the threshold."

Alaina checked for any loose edges of the thick wool blanket around her son. "He's been awake for the past hour and will need a rest soon. Anne should enjoy his company while he is smiling and content to entertain her. He appears pleased to stay in your arms, Devon." Alaina tucked her arm into her husband's, and Charles swung Christian into the air, much to the boy's delight, and settled him at his hip for the short walk into the manor.

Rhona and Anne descended on Devon when he entered the house, and as her husband had predicted, Anne removed the baby from Devon's embrace into her own. "Your sons possess the best of you both." She cooed and placed a feather-light kiss on the baby's nose. Ambrose rewarded her with a gurgling smile. "We set up a nursery next to your room, as the old nursery is closed at the moment. As requested, we have secured the services of one of our maids, Iris, to serve as the boys' nanny while you are here."

"Thank you, Anne, and my apologies again for the inconvenience. My maid married last month, and the boys' nanny at home has a sick father. I did not wish to take her away at Christmas when it will likely be his last. Besides, it is rather an adventure traveling without a contingent of servants."

"Iris is the daughter of one of our tenant farmers, with several younger brothers and sisters. Christian and Ambrose will be well looked after."

Anne handed the baby to Rhona, who in turn held Ambrose close to her breast and shared a loving glance with Charles. "This will be good practice."

Charles smoothed a finger over the baby's face. "It will." He tweaked Christian's nose. "Are you a good big brother?"

Christian nodded and added an emphatic, "Yes," in case anyone was in doubt.

CHAPTER 2

Greyson Hall, Northumberland
December 11, 1782

C andlelight danced near the shadows within while a
tempest wailed beyond the stone walls. Flames
fluttered, and the subtle scent of beeswax mingled with the
rosewater Grace favored after a bath. The white muslin shift
clung to her skin across the shoulders where drops of water
remained.

She twined the string of pearls she wore at their evening
meal, momentarily focused on the gentle clack they made
against the vanity's wooden surface. Dinners were always a
formal affair at the insistence of the earl, her husband of two
years. Night after night, she dressed in the finest silks, sipped
Madeira wine, and listened to her husband turn the plight of
the Revolutionary War onto himself, where he suffered for
the colonials' impudence.

"Alexander is returning home. Perhaps as early as Christmas. This letter is dated three months past."

Grace peered into the dressing-table mirror and watched her husband pace as he read the misplaced letter, delivered into his hands only this evening. "You have missed him."

"You will like him, my dear. Upon his return, we will host a grand reception here at Greyson Hall."

Grace turned to face her husband. "Spencer, dear, Christmas is but a fortnight hence, and it is a dangerous journey to this part of England in such weather. Perhaps in the spring."

"You would deny Alexander the celebration he is due? He fought for England, our interests, and our son's future." Her husband approached from behind, watching her through the mirror rather than looking directly at her. His hands slid over her bare shoulders and brushed aside the heavy locks of fair hair, tickling the base of her neck. "It is what I desire, dear one."

Grace faced the mirror and met Spencer's dark eyes. How did they not burn a hole through the glass and into her skin? His smooth fingertips caressed the sides of her throat and gently turned her face to his. She accepted the press of his warm lips against hers and caught the exhale of his breath before he eased his head, then his body away.

"See it is done." Spencer turned on his heel and walked to his adjoining dressing room.

He expected her to be ready for him, waiting as she always did. "A marriage of happy possibilities," her father once promised before he succumbed to a weak heart one month after her wedding. Too despondent to live as a widow, her mother followed soon after. Whispers among society wondered if Grace's mother realized the ice had not fully formed over the pond that took her life or if she chose that warm winter day to surrender her demons.

Grace rolled one of the delicate pearls between two fingers and stared at the closed door. "Yes, dear. I will see it is done." She gave up her tufted vanity bench for the warmth of the bed. Her body slid beneath the blanket, counterpane, ticking, and cover, drawing each up to her shoulders until they enveloped her enough to ward off winter's chill.

Flames burned low and sparked in the hearth while she waited for her husband. Happy possibilities remained beyond her grasp. Even the fifty thousand pounds she inherited, most of which belonged to her husband now, could not bring about the elusive euphoria her parents once enjoyed. Spencer's handsome features, tall frame, and body lithe from regular exercise should have pleased her enough to overlook a few undesirable qualities, or so her great aunt claimed upon the birth of the Canterbury heir.

Yes, she would see it done. A grand reception, as Spencer wished. People would venture from afar, braving the savage winds and promise of more snow to bask at the firesides of Greyson Hall, for Spencer Canterbury entertained without a sparing thought for pound or pence.

The door's soft creak alerted her that the time for wandering thoughts was at an end. She smiled and turned back the blankets to welcome her husband.

CHAPTER 3

Greyson Hall, Northumberland
December 20, 1892

Fair and golden hair, with eyes of winter blue,
To hold her Highland love beneath the frosted sky;
The Christmas bells ring delicate and true,
Her pale snow whispers, and her bright stars shine.

Alaina and Rhona stood quietly in the hall, listening to the songful tune drifting from the nursery. Iris Gorran, housemaid, now interim nanny, possessed a voice gifted from angels. From their vantage point through the ajar door, they watched Alaina's eldest son's eyes flutter close while her youngest slept to the soothing sounds of Iris's soft ballad.

Where once the babe slept in nurtured arms,
His downy mane truth of beloved and borne;
The silent night nestles once hidden and pure,
And her hushed sigh falls to rest, veiled and shorn.

The lullaby at an end, Alaina entered the room to kiss her sons good night once more. Rhona smoothed a palm over her unborn child and waited beyond the doorway. A draft tickled her neck, and she circled to face the empty hall behind her. Merry laughter she recognized as Devon's drifted from the main level, and her husband's followed. The draft brushed her cheek, this time from the other direction. Rhona peered upward to the ceiling.

"What are you in search of up there?" Alaina's apparent amusement did not trickle over into a full smile. She shuttered the nursery door, leaving an inch of space, and joined Rhona.

"I believe the draft Anne mentioned earlier has found its way into the hall."

Alaina circled her head to look around and up. "I feel nothing."

"It is gone now." Rhona let it go for the moment, intending to inform Devon. "Are you pleased with Iris?"

"She is a godsend." Alaina looped her arm through Rhona's and together they walked down the gallery toward the stairs. "Doubtful she will want to leave and join us at Claiborne Manor, but she'll be a treasure for Anne when she begins her family."

Rhona stopped and rested a hand on Alaina's forearm. "Have you heard something?"

Alaina smiled and lifted her shoulders with affected daintiness as though holding a secret.

"Alaina?"

"No, I have not heard a hint about it, and Devon resigned only two months ago."

Rhona reached the staircase a step before Alaina and clasped the banister before they started down. "I would not be confident bringing a child into this world if Charles still served the crown. I love him for the work he has done and the sacrifices made, yet—"

"I understand." Alaina kept a slow pace down the stairs, for Rhona's sake. "Tristan was away much of the first year of Christian's life, but later . . . Rhona?"

Rhona's fingertips turned white, so fierce was her grip on the railing. "I could have sworn I saw . . ."

"What, dear?"

"I am not entirely sure."

They stood on the step halfway down the staircase. The grand foyer lay before them; besides the noble tree and a few furnishings, nothing existed in the space below. "Rhona, perhaps you should sleep. If you wait here, I will go for Charles."

"No, I am all right." Rhona almost believed her own words. "It is early yet, and I am eager for laughter and perhaps another piece of the delicious cake."

Alaina's straight mouth and drawn eyebrows showed her lack of confidence in Rhona's assurance, yet she smiled, and they proceeded down the rest of the stairs. Before they reached the bottom step, Charles slipped an arm around his wife's waist.

"Are you well, my love?"

Rhona cupped her palm against his face. "Of course I am." She did not miss the worried glance he shared with Alaina. "You have my promise. There is nothing wrong. I am in fine fettle, and though eager to meet our son or daughter, I am more eager for sweets and conversation."

Alaina transferred Rhona's care to Charles and walked ahead of them into the parlor. When they were alone, Charles slowed his steps. "You are unusually pale, Rhona. Do not lie to me, not about this."

She held back a heavy sigh because of his concern. "You will not believe me."

"My dear, I will believe anything you tell me."

"A ghost."

Charles opened his mouth to speak, paused, and studied her. One of his brows raised in a perfect arch. "A ghost?"

"Yes, or a trick of light and shadows."

"Let's go with that."

Rhona leaned up and pressed a kiss to his slight frown. "Or it was a ghost."

Charles's arm remained at her waist with his skepticism firmly in place. When they entered the sitting room, Anne lowered her cup and studied Rhona.

"Are you quite all right, Rhona?"

"She's seen a ghost," Charles helpfully supplied and kissed his wife's cheek when he led her to the empty, red-tufted chair next to Anne's.

"That would explain a few things."

"Pardon?" Devon exited his conversation with Tristan to give his full attention to his wife and Rhona. "The ghost again?"

"Again?" Tristan asked. "Greyson Hall is haunted?"

"No," Devon said.

"Yes," Anne added at the same time. "Devon does not believe me."

"Have you seen a ghost?" Alaina accepted a cup of coffee from the footman and thanked him before he disappeared as quickly as he had appeared. "I would not think it possible, with your uncle the only tenant after its refurbishment. When was it rebuilt?"

"I've acquainted myself with a little of the area's history, including the estate, though a lot is still unknown. Half of the house, primarily what is now the guest wing, burned down in 1793, left to ruin for a decade, then rebuilt. The attics and a portion of the servants' quarters burned in 1842. Much of the structure remained intact, though. Afterward, the estate was purchased by a Lord Percy, who restored the upper levels. He never lived here, and it fell to ruin when his money ran out. That is the version of the house Uncle Wynton bought and refurbished from cellar to attics, except the study. Apparently, he liked the room as it was." Devon sipped from his whiskey.

Charles looked at his wife when he asked Devon, "No report of anyone dying in the fires?"

"One, in the first fire."

Rhona smiled triumphantly at her husband.

"A footman."

Rhona's smile faded. "It is not him."

Devon pressed a fist to his mouth to suppress a chuckle. "The records reported no other unnatural deaths to have occurred here, though they could be wrong. Two fires within the time span is unusual. Foul play? Possible."

"Your uncle lived here six months, was it?" Alaina asked.

Devon nodded. "Yes, though I never knew why. He kept the place in good repair and continued to look after his tenants until his death."

Rhona rested against the chair's back. "You never said where he lived after he left Greyson Hall."

"He traveled between London and Edinburgh, and the former is where he passed." Devon pointed to a modest portrait hanging in an alcove beside a bookshelf. "That's Uncle Wynton there."

"And he did not mention spirits roaming about in his will?" Rhona asked with a hopeful lilt to her voice.

"Sorry, he did not."

"There is the codicil." Anne offered Rhona another cup of tea, though she declined at Anne's words.

Rhona sat up straighter. "What codicil?"

"Not about a ghost." Devon finished his whiskey, his eyes drifting to each doorway during his temporary silence. "About the Gorran family and Christmas Day."

Everyone looked to Anne to decipher. Anne obliged their curiosity. "The Gorran family is to keep their tenancy for as long as they wish, down through the generations. Should the estate sell, their land is to be carved out."

"An unusual arrangement," Tristan mused.

"The estate is not entailed, and the Gorrans are hard workers, so I don't mind." Devon crossed the room to where his uncle's portrait hanged. "He was an eccentric but a good man."

"What about Christmas?" Charles asked.

"Ah." Devon returned to the small gathering. "Anne likes this part."

Anne shifted in her seat and clasped her hands together. "All the tenant farmers are to spend Christmas Day in the hall with the celebration lasting from midday until the entry clock chimes at midnight. He specifically mentioned the Gorran family attend."

"That explains why you made certain to write about the tenant festivities in your invitation." Tristan rested a hand on Alaina's shoulder. "We began a similar celebration on our estate this past summer."

Alaina smiled at her husband, then spoke to Devon and Anne. "You must know none of us mind."

Devon bowed his head to her in gratitude. "Anne knew first, so she claims." He winked at his wife. "It is the tenants I worry about. I am a landowner without a title, which is not as intimidating as a duke and his duchess, or an earl and his countess."

"Your household staff do not appear to catch vapors when we are here."

"They are accustomed to nobility."

Rhona scooted to the front of the chair and sipped at her now lukewarm tea. "Why the Gorran family specifically?"

Devon's chuckle melded with Anne's light laughter. "It has become a game between us," Anne confessed. "The will omits—Rhona?" Anne reached for her friend's hand.

Amusement fled when Rhona bowed her head and breathed deeply. Charles had her standing and secure in his embrace. "Off to bed for us. Too much excitement for your condition."

"Do not fret. Our child will not be born in Anne's parlor." Rhona straightened her back. "It is a slight pain that caught me unawares."

"For my sake, then, let us off to bed." Rhona nodded and clasped Charles's hand. "We're among friends, so please forgive me, darling," Charles added before he swept her into his arms and carried Rhona from the sitting room. Anne hurried to walk before them, assuring Devon all was well and to remain with their guests.

"I am certain the situation is far worse for the men than you ladies can imagine." When Devon turned, he faced Alaina's gaping stare.

Tristan allowed his amusement to show for Devon's benefit. "Got yourself in it now, old friend."

Devon decided the wisest course was to placate Alaina and ignore Tristan. "Of course, we mere men cannot conceive the great suffering you must endure at a time when you must focus all your—"

"Quite all right, Devon." Alaina hid a soft smile with her cup.

Devon released a breath. "Thank you for suffering me."

"I am in a generous state of mind and will consider not telling Anne."

Devon paled, not all his somberness feigned. "And what will tip this generosity in my favor?"

"Your library."

Tristan lowered himself onto the sofa next to his wife. "We have a library, my dear."

"Yes, but while we are here, I want to avail myself of Devon's. Specifically, the tomes and records on the estate's history."

The men shared a look of bemusement. "It is yours, of course, but to what end?" Devon asked. "Of what I have already read, it is a rather dry history."

Alaina kissed her husband, set aside her cup, and rose. "I am going to find Rhona's ghost."

CHAPTER 4

Greyson Hall, Northumberland
December 16, 1782

H e stood an inch taller than the bay Clydesdale's withers, over which he smoothed a gloved hand. His long legs carried him on a smooth stride to the animals' heads, where he whispered to the front pair and rubbed the white markings on their faces.

From where she stood at the window, peering down from the second-level bedroom, Grace watched his every move, her eyes transfixed on the Highlander. Lingering fog, not yet burned off from the morning cold, curled around his trew-clad legs. The leather-trimmed trousers molded what she could see of him beneath his plaid.

Brice Maclean, the only guest from north of Edinburgh on her husband's list of notables he expected to attend. This one held neither title nor lineage of consequence, a rarity among Spencer Canterbury's preferred company.

No other passenger alighted from the gilded four-in-hand coach, a stately and expensive conveyance for a single man of no distinction. Wealth, however, forgave many sins, including a lack of title and position. Grace often believed her husband—contrary to his claims—valued wealth above all else.

The Highlander, Spencer had informed her when she read his name on the guest list, would arrive for business earlier than the other travelers. What enterprise such a man would have with Lord Canterbury of Northumberland remained a mystery, and her husband quelled further inquiry.

Their guest only gave his attention to the earl after speaking with the driver and watching the team drive away toward the stables. Grace wished she knew of what they spoke or read the movements of their lips, but they did not turn their faces upward enough. Only when the earl invited him inside did the Highlander raise his face to gaze upon the stones. A breeze blew his dark hair away from a strong face partially covered in an unfashionable light beard. His eyes pierced her quickly and without apology.

Grace could not credit what kept her at the window with the curtain pulled back, allowing Mr. Maclean to witness her spying upon them. His gaze flitted over her once, then a second time, before leaving her view and entering the house. Under normal circumstances, she would have been downstairs to greet him. However, she quickly discovered nothing about Brice Maclean's arrival was commonplace.

She lingered in the gallery, contemplating, as she often did, the women in the portraits who Spencer called family. Did they love their husbands, or were life and love sacrificed for duty?

His presence came upon her first by his shadow, then by his sigh. Candlelight flickered, and the shadow disrupted the flame's dance on the wall. For such a strapping figure, he moved about with the silence of a slippered lady on carpet.

"Lady Canterbury."

Her head angled so he caught her profile and she a glimpse of his face from her side view. She curved her arms in the direction she wished to turn until a direct and invisible line formed between them.

"Mr. Maclean."

CHAPTER 5

Greyson Hall, Northumberland
December 21, 1892

E lusive sleep and silence kept Rhona from seeking the depth of slumber her mind and body craved. Enclosed in Charles's embrace, she found peace and safety, as always, yet her mind whirled and worked in the early morning hours. When she sensed Charles awaken, Rhona shifted to rest her arm upon his chest and her chin upon her arm. Her waist had not expanded so much as to prevent such a position.

"I have woken you."

Charles smiled before he opened his eyes.

"Not intentionally and not for that purpose."

His smile faded, though never fully disappeared. "You've crushed my hopes." Charles brushed a dark lock over her shoulder. "I could hear you think."

"Also not intentional."

Darkness cloaked the earth beyond the window. A narrow opening in the curtains attested that not even the moon brightened the winter night. Charles wiped both palms over his face and head, mussing his hair even more. "It's the ghost."

"Yes."

Charles lifted himself and moved backward until his back rested against the headboard. He brought Rhona with him and tucked her close. "Tell me about her."

"Beautiful and sad. Her sorrow touched me deeply, Charles, and I cannot explain why." Her fingers made small circles on her husband's chest as the ghost's image floated through her mind. "She stood at the base of the stairs. Long, pale hair flowed down her back and over her shoulders. Her fleeting existence caught us both unawares, of that I am certain."

Charles kissed the top of her head. "You spoke once of a being you saw as a young girl."

"At Davidson Castle. My father thought me mad, but ghosts are common enough in the Highlands, so others in the house believed me. 'Twas a child, a boy close to my age at the time."

"You only saw him once?"

Rhona nodded and found that speaking of it aloud relaxed her. "The woman I saw last evening was perhaps twenty, no more than twenty-five years of age. She bore the mark of such sadness."

"And you know because you have felt such before."

"Aye, though we have all known death and anguish, this was different." She raised herself enough to brush her mouth over his. "You, my love, have cleansed my heart of pain." Rhona pushed the blankets off and dragged herself to the edge of the bed, where she could comfortably shift to climb out.

"Where are you going at this hour?"

An impish grin was Rhona's only response.

"You'll not sleep until you discover who she is, will you?"

Rhona tied the cord at the waist of her flannel dressing gown. The loose garment concealed everything from neck to toes. "You need not come with me."

"Might I convince you to stay here while I search out a few books from Devon's study?"

Rhona merely fluttered her eyelashes.

"Damned if that doesn't work." Charles pushed off the blankets covering his nakedness and dressed in trousers, a loose white shirt, and a housecoat. He slipped into his house shoes before helping Rhona on with her embroidered slippers. "You will find what you want to read, then we'll bring it back to bed. Are we agreed?"

Content that she had her way, Rhona smiled and nodded. The house's silence allowed Rhona to hear the flame's quiver from behind the lamp's glass chimney. Only when they reached the last step did they hear voices. They followed the soft murmurs to Devon's study, where a sliver of light escaped beneath the closed door.

"It would seem you are not the only one with ghosts on your mind, my dear." Charles opened the door, surprising Alaina enough to clasp a hand to her chest.

"A warning next time, Charles, please." Books lay open and papers were strewn across Devon's desk. "We've been found out."

"I'm only surprised it wasn't sooner." Tristan carried a carved wooden box to the desk. "This was behind the books on the house and region's history. We'll leave it for Devon to open at a reasonable hour."

Alaina and Tristan still wore formal evening clothes, though Tristan had removed his dark tailcoat, waistcoat, and tie. A suggestion for Rhona to return to their rooms and dress never parted his lips, for she was already next to Alaina behind the desk.

"What have you found?"

Alaina said, "Devon claimed the history to be dull, and he was right."

Rhona's brow arched in question.

"Oh, he said as much after you'd gone to bed when I asked to avail myself of his library."

"Asked?" Tristan eyed his wife. "You blackmailed him."

Charles shook his head, not at all surprised. Rhona studied her friend in approval. "Well done. Shall I ask with what you blackmailed him?"

"That is easy to conclude." Charles set the lamp on the desk to cast more light across the pages. "She agreed not to repeat something to Anne. Such extortion would work on any of us."

Rhona fixated on her husband. "And what would you want kept silent?"

Charles stared at the walls. "This project would be simpler with electric lights."

"Mm." Rhona returned her attention to the loose papers. "I'd like electricity no better here than at our home, though I daresay the servants would find it useful." Rhona read the writing on the page in her hand as she spoke. "Have you been at this all night?" she asked Alaina.

Tristan answered when his wife only nodded. "She's determined to find your ghost."

"Have you found anything of significance?"

Alaina sighed, lowered herself into Devon's comfortable chair, then stood immediately and pointed to the seat. "You need to rest, not I." Alaina accepted nothing except complete acquiescence.

When Rhona sat, Charles told Alaina, "You'll need to explain one day how you accomplished such a feat."

Tristan and Alaina shared a chuckle at Charles's expense. Rhona did not join the merriment. "This is a letter from an Alexander to Lord Spencer Canterbury. Brothers, I think. It reads that Alexander is returning home after the American Revolution. It is dated September 1782."

Charles asked for the letter and perused what his wife had read. "The peace treaty had yet to been signed in 1782. It would not be until the following year when England affirmed an end to the hostilities."

"Devon said a portion of the house burned in 1793 the first time, so Lord Canterbury may have still lived here."

"Your ghost is a woman, so not Lord Canterbury," Charles pointed out.

Rhona shuffled through more pages, finding nothing else of great interest, at least not to her. "Is this not how you used to research a case?"

Charles and Tristan shared questioning looks over their wives' heads. "We read reports, of course," Tristan said. "We gained most answers from speaking with people, following them, asking questions."

"Spying," Alaina said.

Tristan shrugged and grinned at his wife. "We also slept."

Alaina dropped the papers she'd been looking over. "You are right. We can begin again in the morning." The clock chimed the three o'clock hour. "Or later in the morning, after breakfast."

Tristan and Alaina said good night and left behind the room and the carved box. Charles examined every side of the box, from hinge to lock. "It's well made."

"Can you open it?"

"Without a key?" Charles nodded. "Tristan is right, though. It is for Devon to open. Let us go to bed, Rhona. I promise we will find your ghost."

Rhona leaned forward in the chair and rested her

forearms on the papers strewn across the desk. "Tristan said you spoke with people and asked questions to solve your cases."

"You've witnessed how we work, and that *is* often how it gets done. People hold more clues than history texts."

"Then I must speak with Anne at breakfast."

Charles helped his wife stand and started the slow walk from the room. "What do you expect Anne to know?"

"Nothing, at least not about this. I need to speak with her before approaching someone who may already know the ghost's identity."

Rhona's unborn child proved tired and claimed hours of sleep more than Rhona had been prepared to give. Gray clouds kept all except the most eager sunlight from shining through the window. With curtains drawn open at both windows, snow-covered hills and a single rider entered Rhona's view. The man rode away from the house. Rhona recalled one of the tenant farms lay beyond the first hill.

She lifted her head enough to peek over the coverlet when Charles entered from the bathing chamber. "You did not wake me."

Charles smiled at the accusation. "Were it not necessary for our child to eat, I would not wake you now. Sleep is good for you."

Rhona pulled him toward her when he sat beside her and kissed him thoroughly. "You are lucky we love you so much."

"A gift I give thanks for daily." Charles kissed her again, then leaned back and studied her face. "Is it love for me, food, or learning more about the ghost that has made you so agreeable? No, do not answer." He left her to remove herself from bed and returned to her side without asking when she needed assistance with her morning dress of silk, gauze, and velvet. She had given up the bustle long before it grew out of fashion, and though one of London's finest modistes altered her gowns to fit Rhona's expanding waistline, she still had some room to spare for additional comfort.

Charles nuzzled her neck and whispered, "Never has a woman been more beautiful."

Rhona indulged in her husband's attention for several minutes until he'd left her breathless—and distracted.

"Your antics, though appreciated and welcome, will not work."

He smiled against her lips and sighed. "To breakfast then."

Anne and Alaina were still seated when they reached the breakfast room, their plates half full of the kitchen's morning offerings. Charles pulled out a chair for his wife and once she was seated, walked to the sideboard to fill a plate for Rhona.

"Alaina told me of your early-morning research." Anne waited until a footman served Rhona cocoa before continuing. "She mentioned a letter you found addressed to Lord Canterbury."

Rhona sipped at the cocoa and thanked Charles when he set a plate before her, though her eyes widened at the fare: sausages, bacon, eggs, and bread rolls with preserves, enough to feed two grown men. She thought the eggs safe and started there. "Yes, do you know of Lord Canterbury?"

"Only what Devon has learned. Parish records show he lived here when his wife disappeared. He disbanded the servants, locked up the house, and moved to Surrey, where it's said he lost his mind. No one saw or heard from him since. We know little else or even how much of that is true. It is all village talk that has passed down the generations."

"What of the boy and his wife, his son's mother?"

Anne shook her head. "The son reportedly went to live with a cousin in Scotland, then lived in London in his later years. There is no mention of a wife in any will, tome, or paper we have found thus far, but there are a century of books and documents to scour. Derek has not relished going through it all. I think the church where the Canterburys were likely married and their son christened burned as well, during a skirmish between two crofting families in 1789. All records prior to that year were lost."

Rhona glanced at her plate again and noticed she'd eaten through the eggs, sausage, and half a roll. Her unborn child rested comfortably and quietly, earning her gratitude. If all it took was a good meal to minimize the kicking, she would eat her weight in food daily.

"Rhona?"

She looked up to find all three of her breakfast companions watching her. "Has Alaina told you about the box?"

The women smiled, and Anne nodded. "She just mentioned it. Devon and Tristan have gone to look over a new racer Devon purchased last month."

Charles wiped his mouth with a flannel serviette and kissed his wife on the cheek before rising. "I believe I'll join them at the stables and leave you ladies to your plotting."

Alaina finished her cocoa, and when they no longer heard his footsteps, she said, "Such things are better left to the women."

Laughing, Anne nodded to the butler that they'd finished. "If we go to the study now, we can resume the search. Perhaps additional letters will offer clues."

"The children already adore Iris, so I have—"

Rhona stopped short in the hall. "I'd forgotten. Anne, would you mind if I spoke with Iris?"

"It is her permission you will need, but why?"

"Because a woman haunts your house, and Iris Gorran may know why."

CHAPTER 6

Greyson Hall, Northumberland
December 18, 1782

Wind caressed and rushed over her face, whipping hair from the mass of unpowdered curls beneath her broad-brimmed hat. Her heartbeats raced in time with the mare's hoofbeats until Grace slowed the horse to a steady canter and then a stop.

They stood near the shadow of the tall oak that guarded the hilltop and listened to the breeze sing through frost-touched branches. During the summer and autumn, she found solace beneath the tree, its lobed-shaped leaves providing shelter from the sun. The great oak's branches now swayed above its fallen leaves, and the winter sun hid behind dark, featureless clouds covering half the sky. One side dark, the other still light. At the end of this day, she wondered which side she would be under.

"More snow is coming."

How did she not see him approach or hear his horse move in from behind? Though they no longer ran across the land, Grace's heart beat a foreboding tune. "Before the hour is over." Why then did she not leave and seek shelter at home with her husband?

Brice Maclean walked his horse in front of her, then turned the steed around to face Grace, a mere foot apart. "Yer an impressive rider."

"You do not sound Scots." Grace didn't know why she said such a thing. "Or rather, your English is quite good."

Brice's laugh surprised her, and though it dissipated, his smile did not. "No' in England. Ye wouldnae underston me."

"I understand fine, Mr. Maclean." She was grateful the cold hid the rising heat in her face. "That is not Gaelic."

"Nae. It is not. Business often takes me to London, and I lack a title, making my Scots tongue difficult to bear."

Grace enjoyed his strong and husky voice, the voice of a confident man who knew what to say and meant what he said, be damned the consequences. She did not bring up his wealth, which is undoubtedly why her husband welcomed him. "You have never been here to Greyson Hall."

Brice shook his head and without warning, dismounted. He dropped the horse's reins over its neck and held both hands up to Grace. "Give the mare a rest."

She shouldn't get off the horse, slide into his arms, or imprint forever to her memory the warmth of his body despite the frigid air. Yet, she did all three before sense convinced her otherwise. With her feet secure upon the ground, Grace stepped away.

She covered her mouth to clear her throat before she could speak. "Why are you here, Mr. Maclean?"

"If I tell ye, will ye call me Brice?"

"If you do not want to say, then do not."

His laugh again, seductive and unnerving in equal measure. "Lord Canterbury has requested my counsel."

Grace contemplated him from beneath the hat's brim. "Counsel regarding what exactly?"

"That I cannot say, my lady."

"You should not trust him." Her whispered words were so soft Grace heard them only in her mind. She hoped the earth and sky had carried them away before reaching the Highlander's ears.

"Tell me, Lady Canterbury." His fingers brushed her woolen cloak, and the burn of his touch reached her skin. "Why should I not trust your husband?"

Her words snagged on a breath, and she held the rest back, only to shake her head.

Brice leaned close behind the tree's protective trunk. How had they moved without her realizing it? "Do not."

"Do not what?"

Grace curved her body toward him and raised her face to peer into his eyes and discern his true measure. He was not smiling now, nor did he bring her closer to him or he to her. "Why are you in Northumberland?"

"It is beautiful here, and your husband sent an invitation."

She pushed him away. "Leave now before I say something I will regret come tomorrow."

"Why are you angry?"

His calmness did nothing to ease her ire. "Why do you provoke me with such intention? If you have nothing to say in answer to my questions, then leave, or I shall leave." Grace's departure was halted by firm hands on her shoulders. They held her with purpose and protection rather than force. She tried to reason how she knew the difference from this man.

"You said I should not trust your husband." The curls

above her ear fluttered from his warm breath. "What has he done, Lady Canterbury, to lose your trust?"

CHAPTER 7

Greyson Hall, Northumberland
December 21, 1892

"Fair and golden hair, with eyes as winter blue."

"From the lullaby, my lady?"

Rhona smiled. "Yes, and a lovely lullaby it is. Do you know its origins?"

"It's a legend, my lady, from long ago."

Rhona lowered herself into the most comfortable of the three chairs in the room, set up to watch children at play. Much to Iris's surprise, Alaina put herself at level with the children on the carpet, holding baby Ambrose while Christopher toppled homemade wooden blocks for the second time. Iris deftly helped him stack the blocks again while speaking with Rhona.

"A legend of what?"

"Why, the Lady of Greyson Hall."

Anne shook her head when Rhona glanced her way. "I have never heard of such a legend."

"It's an old one, my lady." Iris held two blocks in her hand and tweaked Christopher's nose when he chose one, put it back, then chose the other. "My mum told me, and her mum before her. No one believes it, not really."

Rhona needed someone to believe the tale, at least enough to ensure she wasn't going mad.

"Iris," Anne said. "Would your mother mind a visit this afternoon? We wouldn't want to inconvenience her."

"That's kind of you, my lady, and she'd consider it an honor. She'll be here, though, to deliver the blaa buns you wanted, my lady."

"Your mother makes those?" Anne gave a genuine smile to Iris. "Never have I had anything so wonderful since I left Ireland. I incorrectly assumed our chef made them."

Iris returned the smile. "My mum has a way with blaa buns. The recipe passed from my father's mother."

"I have been craving more food from my homeland lately, and the blaa buns are my favorite. I will be certain to thank your mother when I see her."

Hesitantly, Iris said, "It wouldn't be right for me to fetch her to you when she comes. Might I tell Mr. Hatch, my lady?"

"Of course, that will be fine and appreciated." Anne nodded toward the children. "Thank you, again, for acting as a nanny over the holidays."

"It's a pleasure and honor, truly." Iris bobbed her head at Alaina. "Truly, Your Grace, they're such good lads."

"I think so, too." Alaina smiled at Iris before she held out an arm for Christopher's hug, kissed the top of Ambrose's head, and passed the baby to Iris before deftly getting to her feet. "Thank you, Iris, for your care and time."

Anne and Alaina started to leave, and Rhona begged for

a moment alone with Iris. "I will be right along." Once alone, Rhona asked Iris, "This is a rather unorthodox question, and you do not have to answer."

"I'll help any way I can, my lady."

"Has your family spent Christmas at the hall before?"

Iris shook her head once, then nodded before shrugging. "I haven't, my lady, but my mum and grandmother did when Mr. Clayton lived here. I mean, Mr. Wynton Clayton."

"Did they?" With help from the armrests, Rhona lifted herself from the plush chair. "Please, do not stand on my account," Rhona added when Iris went to her knees. "I'll leave you now to enjoy yourselves." She smoothed a hand over her unborn child and immediately saw the ghost's sorrowful eyes in her mind.

Rhona joined Anne and Alaina in the hall and perceived that they had overheard her conversation with Iris. "Let's not speak of it here."

They removed themselves to Anne's parlor, where their hostess called for tea. "Now, while we are waiting, tell us what is bothering you, Rhona."

"Anne is right." Alaina sat next to Rhona on a settee. "This began as a fun hunt for a ghost, but you are out of sorts."

"It's her, the spirit. If she is Lady Canterbury, how is it she is barely a memory? She had a child, a son. It is beyond comprehension that a mother would leave her son behind unless circumstances gave her no choice."

The conversation paused as a footman carried in a silver tray laden with a tea service for three. "Thank you, Oscar. I will serve."

"Very good, ma'am. I mean, my lady." The young footman bowed and left the room, closing the door behind him.

"He is new?" Rhona accepted the teacup from Anne with gratitude.

Anne nodded. "Oscar arrived one week ago. He is the son of one of our tenants, though he prefers service to farming. He is not yet used to calling Devon Mr. Clayton and me Lady Clayton. I expect it sounds wrong to him."

"Devon insisted you retain your title, as is your right," Alaina said. "I recall in the early days when I first met Devon, he cared nothing for any of it. He called me Alaina, and it never sounded wrong."

"We have all forgone titles amongst ourselves. It is perhaps odd to any servant." Rhona sipped the tea and raised her eyes to Anne. "Heather and thistle?"

"I asked our cook to stock it for when you visit." Anne added milk to her cup and stirred it before taking her seat. "I have taken a liking to it. Now, what else do you remember about the ghost?"

"Do you believe she exists?" Rhona asked.

"I am not a stranger to ghosts, so yes, I do. Other than a drafty nursery, there has been no sign of one, so we must rely on you."

Alaina set her cup aside. "The original nursery, not the one the children are in?"

"The original," Anne assured her. "I thought it best to close it up, but why would that room be haunted?"

Rhona finished her tea and stood. "Alaina, Devon gave you carte blanche to use his study, did he not?"

Alaina's eyes brightened. "He certainly did."

"Then back to the study, and we will need Devon's help, Anne."

Anne followed her friends from the room. "I say, Rhona. You would have made a superb agent."

❄

"You're losing your flair, old chap." Tristan and Devon watched as Charles picked the lock to the wooden chest.

Charles straightened the arch in his back and stretched his shoulders. "I am working under the assumption that Devon does not want the box damaged. The hinges and lock plate are genuine silver, and the carvings are the work of a master."

"Uncle Wynton's papers say nothing of the box or its contents. He was not a man of secrets, at least to hear my father tell it." Devon tapped the top of the desk. "I searched every compartment in this desk when I first moved in and never came across a key that would fit that lock."

"Then be so good as to be quiet." Charles returned to the lock. He closed his eyes, slowed his breathing, and listened to the sound of the prying tip click against the mechanism within. "Were Alfred Hobbs still in England, we'd have been through—Ah. There it is."

The lock clicked, and the latch released. "The first look is yours, Devon."

"Well done." Devon took Charles's place in front of the box.

Tristan crossed his arms and waited for Devon to raise the lid. "By the by, Charles, Hobbs died last year in America."

"Did he? I am losing my touch. Did he leave a protégé?"

"Not that the agency has concerned themselves with." Tristan shrugged. "Retirement does not negate the need to remain informed, and exceptional lock pickers are worth knowing about. Are you going to open the box, Devon?"

"The ladies ought to be here."

"I prefer to spare Rhona the disappointment if nothing in there offers a clue to her ghost or rather, your ghost." Charles motioned upward with his finger.

"On your own head be it." Devon raised the lid and let it

fall backward toward the desktop. "Now, I think we should call in our wives."

"No need, darling." Anne swept her arm with an exaggerated flourish in front of herself and her friends standing in the doorway. "We are already here."

"Anne." Devon grinned, closed the box, and approached his wife to kiss her mouth. "My darling beloved." When he failed to move her, he peered at his friends. "All yours." Devon clasped his wife's hand and gently encouraged her to follow him back to the desk. "Rhona, you'll want to see this as well."

Charles had already circled his wife's back with a supporting arm. "Promise me you won't be upset if a clue about your ghost does not exist in the box."

Rhona tipped her head back, her expression incredulous. "Charles, we really must speak about your overprotective behavior of late. I am with child, not riding horseback with a sword at my hip to fight in battle."

"Although that might be fun," Alaina said, adding a wink for her husband.

"Perish the thought, my love." Tristan returned her wink and pointed to the box. "Devon, the suspense is fast losing its grip on us."

"Speak for yourself." Anne poked a finger in her husband's side. "Though, do get on with it, please."

Devon once more lifted the lid, then stepped aside and nodded to Rhona. "The honor is yours."

Rhona tentatively ran a finger over the thin leather-bound volume and the soft leather ties that bound it closed. A single scratch crossed the top right corner, but the book was otherwise without etching or blemish. "It's too new, too soft, to be hers."

"Don't give up yet. My father may have often referred to Uncle Wynton as reckless and devoid of responsibility, but he possessed a sharp mind. If this was already here, then he found it and read it. Look, the leather tie is a different color, darker and less faded than the rest."

Rhona lifted the book from the box and gently tugged at the careful bow. The spine cracked a little when she turned back the cover. Words written upon the first page, in a pristine English round hand, made her hands tremble.

All is dead in a world not of my choosing, except the life I now carry inside of me. It alone is the light in a darkness that will stay the cudgel in my hand. This account will prove my folly should I ever find the courage again.

Charles's warm breath caressed her neck as he read the words over her shoulder. "Well, that's cheery."

Rhona reread the words aloud for the others. "She was going to kill someone. Is that not what it says?"

"That is how I read it." Charles flipped to the next page. "Same handwriting." He continued to skim his fingers over the page edges. "And it looks to be at least half filled."

"She was going to kill her husband, or I am guessing it is him." At Rhona's widened eyes, Tristan shrugged and continued. "The child she carried stopped her, but she still wanted to. Your ghost may not be as innocent as you think."

"It might not be her, the spirit I saw." Rhona closed the journal. "It could have been anyone." Except, Rhona knew, in the depths of trembling heart, that the woman in spirit and the woman on the page were the same.

CHAPTER 8

Greyson Hall, Northumberland
December 20, 1782

B aron Whitford arrived next with a manservant, and Lord Bowley arrived soon after without one. Both widowers, both men of great wealth, and Grace knew nothing about either save their position and power.

Alexander, the brother-in-law she had yet to meet, remained absent in body and silent in word. She sensed her husband's anxiousness, though he acted as a generous host to the remainder of their guests, who arrived slowly over two days, with three more expected before Christmas Eve.

"Business before pleasure," her husband had said about the early arrivals. Spencer Canterbury was gentle in his command of what he expected, and Grace never mistook the gentleness for affection.

Four wives had accompanied their husbands, and each one appeared quite content to be ignored by the men, though Grace suspected two of the couples shared an honest love, and it was to these women she felt drawn, for a time at least.

They laughed and gossiped and spoke of all the mind-numbing events from the last London season that they still found amusing for some unfathomable reason. Her husband's business spared Grace the obligatory balls and dinners. Invitations still came when one lived in the far north, but there was no surprise when they were declined.

She needed to breathe, to think, to be anywhere doing anything except listening to the chatter. Grace performed her duty as the lady of the house through dinner and drinks until the clock struck an hour suitable to retire.

Her husband brought her close as the couples and bachelors withdrew to their respective bedchambers. "I will join you later, Grace. Lord Whitford and I have business."

He gave her time to murmur her accord and silently thank Lord Whitford for the diversion. Even the Highlander had joined in the mundane talk throughout the evening. She had thought better of him.

Desperation to be alone propelled Grace to the solarium off the great hall. It was her favorite room in the manor, rarely used except by her. Exotic plants in extravagant pots dotted the glass-encased room, and beyond the floor-to-ceiling windows, darkness engulfed all but the layer of sparkling snow covering the grounds.

"You never answered my question, Lady Canterbury."

Her eyes closed, and she sucked in a quiet breath.

"Two days ago, when you ran away. Surely you remember."

He stood closer now. How did he move without making a sound on the dark marble floor? She recalled he had left the parlor before her. Did he know the direction of her thoughts, or had he also sought solace in the quiet space? "You shouldn't be in here."

"We are safe, I assure you. It is too cold for anyone else to venture into an unlit room."

"I find the cold comforting."

"What has your husband done to lose your trust?"

She heard him whisper from barely a foot behind her. His soft and lulling voice held a layer of his native Scots and for a moment she did not think or move. When her thoughts returned under her control, she wondered why she did not turn or walk away. Even as her mind pondered, her traitorous body remained rooted in place. "I did not answer you because such a question does not deserve a response." She did turn then, much to her regret. The heat from his body warmed her as no hearth fire could, and the emerald glint in his eyes darkened as they roamed her face.

"Why should I not trust your husband? You may not have meant to speak the words, yet you did."

Grace tilted her head and studied his face. She made no move to back away. "Your business matters with my husband are no concern of mine."

"Then why warn me?"

"You are far too curious in matters that have no meaning for you." She forced her eyes to remain open when she longed to close them and awaken from the nightmare of her own making. "Forget I spoke."

"I cannot do that." Brice's eyes narrowed, and he closed another six inches between them. Still, she did not retreat. "Why are you not afraid of me?"

"How can you be certain I am not?"

"You tremble when I am near," he whispered, "yet there is no fear in your eyes. You hide the fear well with him but not well enough."

How long would she live a lie? Grace nearly choked the

words back before she finally spoke them. "When one lives with a monster, nothing is left to fear, not beyond him." Brice raised a hand to palm her face. Neither soft, nor too rough, his were the hands of a man familiar with work, but one who did not toil in labor. She rubbed her smooth cheek against his hand before she considered the consequences. "What do you want, Mr. Maclean?"

His hand caressed the other cheek, and he drew her toward him. "Everything I shouldn't." Their hearts beat faster, the sound of both combining and rising above the rhythm of their breaths.

Brice's fingers drifted over her skin, smoothing down her neck, until they circled her nape and brought her closer. He grazed her with his eyes until his penetrating stare touched every inch of visible flesh. It wasn't enough, and she knew that when this man kissed her, when their bodies found a way to come together, no force would dare pull them apart. Grace met and held his eyes, unwilling to give him a reason not to follow through with the promise they held.

"The oath be damned." He muttered the curse a second before the warm press of lips that tasted of brandy and forbidden hope. She craved and clung to his jacket, welcoming the gentle onslaught and encouraging more. His arms encircled and urged her as near to him as the arms pressed between them allowed.

On another curse, he jerked away, only to pull her back and kiss her again, this time with a promise to possess. She sensed his withdrawal before his embrace loosened, and he distanced himself from her touch.

Grace did not want to give him the satisfaction of knowing how fully his kiss had consumed her, yet she could not stop her fingers from touching her tingling lips or halt the rise and fall of her chest with each ragged breath. "You will not ask my forgiveness."

His own shaky breath joined hers. "I want no forgiveness, for there is no regret."

She gained comfort from seeing a storm in his eyes, similar to the one she felt still raging within. "What oath?" Brice shook his head and fisted both hands at his sides. Grace found a store of strength and stepped toward him. "I have a right to know what stopped you."

Brice skimmed a hand over her arm. "Discipline stopped me. I cannot guarantee it will do so again. He will not come to you tonight."

Grace did not have to ask who Brice meant. "He will."

"Not tonight. Never again."

"Oath or not?" Grace trailed a finger over his chest. "What are you to Spencer Canterbury?"

Brice covered her hand, stopping its movement. "Don't ask what I cannot tell you."

"Whatever it is he wants from you, he will get it—or see you dead."

His lips brushed hers once, slowly. "You bestow him with too much power."

Grace walked into his arms. "He is a beast who will tear apart every foe without bloodying his own hands."

"I know." Brice rested his chin atop her head and smoothed a hand over the pale, silky strands. "It is why I am here."

CHAPTER 9

Greyson Hall, Northumberland
December 21, 1892

"Have you read anything to suggest your ghost is not a murderer?"

Rhona shook her head at Alaina's question. "She is the ghost, so I daresay it is her who met an ill fate."

"Yes, but why I wonder." Anne rose and walked to the parlor window, where they had retired to, leaving their husbands in Devon's study. "Derek and Zachary are late, and the sky is angry enough to promise a storm."

"They have traveled in worse weather." Alaina joined her friend at the expansive window and studied the landscape in companionable silence.

"She writes of a Highlander."

"What is that, Rhona?" Anne asked.

Rhona glanced at each friend, taking a few seconds to clear her mind. "What? Oh, the Highlander. Listen."

. . .

*Tall of stature, broad of shoulder, and thick of hair. The
Highlander is rarely without half a smile, as though he knows
something about me I do not. When he arrived today, Lord
Canterbury afforded him great generosity of his time and
whisked this man into his study without an introduction. Were
it not for his brazenness, the circumstances of our meeting
would have lacked . . . no, I cannot write what I cannot think
to describe. He stirs me as no other, and this with a mere glance.
He needs to stay away from me, and I from him.*

"She sounds infatuated and only having met him." Alaina
mused her words over. "Of course, I thought the same of
Tristan. He infuriated me, but I found him no less attractive
for it."

"Same with Devon when I first met him," Anne said.
"My mind was certainly on other matters, yet he captivated
me from almost the first. It was the same for you, Rhona, for
us all. We can certainly understand a woman falling under
fascination's spell. And she despised her husband."

"Yes," Rhona agreed. "She goes on later again about
him."

*The Highlander is not who he seems, of this and little else I
am certain. I am suffocating; he is the air I need to fill my
lungs. My son, my beloved Hartley, should not know a father
such as the one who shares his blood, yet there is no hope for it.
I am assured there is hope, though, and cleave unto it with a
desperation heretofore unknown.*

. . .

"It is incredibly sad." Alaina sat next to Rhona and held out her hands. "May I?"

Rhona passed the journal a moment before the butler entered the room and announced Mrs. Gorran's arrival.

"Will you please show her up, Hatch?"

"To the parlor, my lady?"

Anne smiled at the hint of surprise and snobbery in his voice. "Yes, to the parlor, and see tea is brought in."

Hatch bowed his head before making his exit.

"Poor man. He mourns my lack of decorum at times. He does not expect as much from Devon because he was born without a title, which I find tiresome. Devon finds it amusing." Anne shook her head and walked to the hearth to stand near its warmth. "Ireland by the sea was never so cold as this." Her gaze drifted again to the window, and the beginnings of fresh snow fluttered to earth.

"Why are you worried about Devon's brothers?" Rhona asked. "You never have before."

"Not worried," Anne corrected. "Eager for their arrival. Of course, Devon has not spoken of it as he does not know the details, but he was an agent long enough to know when a case is particularly troubling."

Alaina looked up from the journal. "Are they in more danger than usual?"

"When Devon does not think I am watching him, he checks his timepiece, and I glimpse a bleakness. It has been this way since a messenger arrived with a note from Derek the day before you arrived. He has not heard from Zachary in a sennight, though both brothers assured us they would be here."

"If he—" Whatever Rhona was going to say was interrupted by Mrs. Gorran's arrival. Hesitant to enter the parlor, the guest smoothed the skillfully woven shawl she wore over a tailored bodice and gray wool skirt covering her petite frame.

"You asked for me, my lady?"

Anne held out a hand in welcome and crossed to stand beside Iris Gorran's mother. "Please forgive me if I have worried you with my request to have you join us. I hope it is not an inconvenience."

"Not at all, my lady."

"I believe you met Lady Blackwood and the Duchess of Wadebrooke at the village fair this past summer."

"Indeed. It was good of you all to come and support us." Mrs. Gorran bowed her head. "Iris, my lady, she told me what this visit might be about. The Canterbury legend."

The footman arrived, causing a pause in the conversation. He set out the tea and sandwiches and left quietly.

"Yes, Iris mentioned you might know more about it than she could share." Anne motioned for the woman to sit, and after another hesitation, Mrs. Gorran settled on the edge of a tufted chair. Anne poured and served her tea, and she was surprised enough to accept it. "It is an odd request, I know, but we have a bit of a mystery on our hands and desire to solve it before Christmas."

"Oh, I don't think you'll solve it before then, my lady. Pardon my impertinence."

"Why is that?" Rhona asked.

"Well, my lady, if 'tis about the ghost, she never leaves. Been here since my grandmother and her mother before."

"What of during the renovations? Were there no known sightings?" Anne pointed out. "A spirit must have a house to, well, haunt, I suppose."

"She came back after each fire, my lady, or so the story is told."

"Do you know nothing more about it other than what is in the ballad?" Alaina asked, returning the journal to Rhona.

Mrs. Gorran sipped her tea and accepted a sandwich when Anne offered. With each question about the legend, she appeared more at ease. "Many have tried to solve the mystery, thinking that solving it would send Lady Canterbury into the next life, as is proper. It's not right, her spending a century in between worlds."

Rhona gripped the closed journal on her lap. "And none have come close to discovering what happened to her?"

Mrs. Gorran shook her head. "It's believed if the truth were known, she would have left. She comes every year for a fortnight before Christmas, and no one sees her again until the next year. In the years when parts of the manor lay in rubble, no one knows where she went. Of course, my lady, with no one living in the big house, we can't rightly say for sure if she was here or not."

"Have you seen her?" Rhona asked before she thought better of it.

The slow nod this time was done in reverence. "Yes, my lady, once when I was newly married. My family has been at Privet Farm for generations. I've no brothers, so Mr. Gorran took over the tenancy from my father."

Rhona attempted to follow the ancestral line from Lady Grace Canterbury, Countess of Greyson Hall to Mrs. Gorran, wife of a tenant farmer. She understood how such things happened, and did not have to ask when Mrs. Gorran next volunteered the information.

"Lady Canterbury's son, Hartley Canterbury, sired three children, the youngest a girl who married a land agent on her eighteenth birthday. Her father gifted them with Privet Farm. It is through their union my grandmother was born."

Anne took up the chair next to Mrs. Gorran. "It would seem you have more claim to this land than we do."

Mrs. Gorran quickly shook her head. "No, my lady. I would never suggest it. No claim at all except to the land we work and love. It is told Lady Canterbury never thought of Greyson Hall as her home, so we never have. She is a long time in the past, and ghosts or no, we have living to do."

Impressed with the woman, Rhona smiled at her and asked, "You are a credit to your ancestor."

Mrs. Gorran's shrewd study of Rhona lasted seconds before she declared in a whisper-soft voice, "You're the one then who has seen her."

"How did you know?"

"It's in the eyes, Lady Blackwood. Whoever sees her carries a touch of her sadness in them." Mrs. Gorran set aside her teacup, though she made no move to stand. She addressed Anne when she said, "My lady, I don't know what any of you can do that hasn't already been tried, but if you can help her, my family would be indebted."

"Point of curiosity." Alaina resettled closer to the edge of the settee. "What has been tried?"

Mrs. Gorran chuckled a little, though it sounded more like bafflement than humor. "Séances, healers who claim to work magic, even a garden built in her name in hopes to lure her away from the house. The last attempt was made when my grandmother was a girl. We've left the ghost alone since."

"Well, Mrs. Gorran." Rhona shared a look of determination with Anne and Alaina. "We do not know any magic workers, but we do know three men who have never failed to solve a mystery."

When Mrs. Gorran took her leave, with another thank you from Anne for the delicious bread, Charles poked his head into the parlor, and finding it clear of visitors, strode to his wife's side. It was to the other women he asked, "Is she well?"

Rhona tugged on his arm. "You can ask me."

"You would lie, my dear." Charles returned his gaze to Anne and Alaina.

"She is the picture of health," Anne assured him before she tugged the bellpull in the corner.

Charles plucked a tea sandwich off the tray. "Was your visitor of any help?"

"I suppose it depends on how one defines help." Alaina poured fresh tea into Rhona's cup. "If you mean in the usual way, then no."

"Unless, of course, you know someone capable of performing a séance."

Charles's hand hovered above a second sandwich when he peered down at his wife. "I can see you are not serious." He narrowed his gaze. "Or are you?"

"I lie, my dear. You should ask one of them." Rhona waved a hand to indicate her friends.

"Deserved that." Charles forgot the sandwich and pressed a kiss to his wife's brow. "What did Mrs. Gorran say about your ghost?"

"As it happens, she is not *my* ghost."

CHAPTER 10

Greyson Hall, Northumberland
December 21, 1782

S he longed to remove her stay, to release a long breath without the heavy boning pressing into her flesh. The false graciousness she'd managed thus far wavered when Alexander Canterbury alighted from his frost-covered coach and entered Greyson Hall.

The guest of honor had finally arrived.

His homecoming interrupted a vast breakfast buffet, which delayed the planned indoor games and other amusements, including charades and whist for the ladies and the promise of friendly gambling for the men, a cover, Grace suspected, for talk of business.

Alexander resembled his brother in almost every way. They were of the same height, three inches shorter than six feet, with hair the color of dark wheat and sky-colored eyes, though lacking the hopeful glint of the sun's warmth.

To say she hated him would simplify her feelings toward her brother-in-law. A peacock if ever one existed, and beneath his plumage, a hard resentment toward his brother and a stomach-wrenching lust for her.

Grace did not think her husband saw the looks that led her to these feelings, but she did. Breakfast moved into luncheon and luncheon into tea. Grace did not believe herself capable of averting one more of Alexander's glances.

"Are you quite all right?"

It took Grace a moment to realize one of the wives was speaking to her. She did not know which one, so she simply nodded. "Whist is not my game."

The women laughed, as Grace knew they would. She did not share their amusement. The dressing gong sounded at seven o'clock, releasing her, however temporarily, from her hostess cage. She escaped to the solarium and clawed at her bodice, but too much fabric lay between her hands and the stay.

"You are avoiding me, sister."

Grace wrenched her arm away and stumbled three steps before circling to face Alexander. "Do not touch me."

He held up his arms as if to ward off her accusation. "I merely sought to help you." Alexander glanced over his shoulder. "We share an affection for the darkness, dear sister."

"Your brother will be looking for you."

Alexander's lips curved. "My dear brother is much too engrossed with business to notice my absence." He advanced. "Tell me, sister, how did my brother catch such a prize?"

"If you do not leave, I will."

He sidestepped to block her path. "Spencer owes me a debt. Did you know that?"

Grace frowned. "What debt?"

"So, he did not tell you."

"What debt, Alexander?"

"That is between me and my brother. As he does not have the means to repay it, I have chosen how he will discharge his debt."

Grace prayed for a knife to appear in her hand, even as she sought an alternative path from the solarium. Could she reach the door to the snow-covered patio before he caught her? Did she care if her screams would cause a scandal unlike any she and her husband would survive? Grace chose to find safety in the snow and cold beyond the glass door. Her slippered feet carried her faster and farther than she thought capable, though she stopped short of her destination, with her hand ready to turn the handle. When the screech came, however, it was not from her lips.

Brice's stare held steady above Alexander's writhing form, and only after he'd roamed his eyes over her from hem to hair did he look away. Brice dragged Alexander to the nearest wall and slammed him face-first against it before spinning him around. When Alexander started to shout, Brice's hand clamped over his mouth.

"You'll not say a word. Do you understand?"

Alexander nodded and tried to push Brice away.

"If you're after a broken limb, that's the way to go about it."

Alexander stopped moving except for the heady rise and fall of his chest.

"The lady does not want what you are offering. Do you agree?"

A darted glance at Grace had Alexander hesitating before he nodded.

"And you will never go near her again."

It was not posed as a question, but Alexander once more agreed. Brice released him, stepping back in a way to stand between Alexander and Grace.

Alexander scrambled along the wall until he ran into a potted palm and quickly moved around it. "My brother will hear of this. You will be gone tonight."

"Would you like to learn what will happen if you speak of this to anyone?"

Grace could not see Brice's face, but there was no mistaking the amusement in his voice—or the fear etched on Alexander's countenance.

"I thought not. Leave. Now."

Several seconds passed before Brice faced her. She remained grounded near the glass doors, unafraid, yet uncertain of the man whose gentle caress contradicted his present behavior.

"My husband favors his brother."

"Above you?"

Grace did not need to voice what she could say with a darting glance to avoid Brice's direct gaze. "Thank you."

He moved silently, so much that Grace barely looked up, and he was standing before her. "Will you leave this place?"

She stared up at him. "Will you go with me?"

"I cannot." It cost him to say the words.

She pressed. "Then why ask if I will go?"

"You and your son are not safe here."

Grace did not need to be told what she already knew. She remained for the same reason she longed to leave. "Such things are not for you to say or determine on my behalf." She pushed him away, and he went, though not from the force of her meager strength against his warrior's body. Her skirts brushed his legs as she passed.

Brice stood in place, watching—hoping—for her return. However, the footsteps on the hallway carpet did not belong to his lady. A footman appeared in the dark entrance, framed by candlelight behind him.

"Mr. McLean, sir. Lord Canterbury asks for you in his study."

Brice nodded once to acknowledge the message, and when he did not move, the footman retreated. Alexander Canterbury, sniveling fool that he was, had not betrayed what transpired between them, which meant Brice's patience may soon be rewarded.

CHAPTER 11

Greyson Hall, Northumberland
December 21, 1892

L ate afternoon brought a break in the snow and a commotion at the front entrance of Greyson Hall.

"Not fit for man or beast out there." Zachary Clayton brushed a few flakes from his overcoat before shrugging out of it.

"Let us hope we can charm a warm meal and drink from the kitchen." Derek also removed his coat and hat, and the brothers handed both to the patient butler. "What do you say, Hatch? Are the others about?"

"They are, sir."

"And you're late." Devon grinned when he sauntered into the foyer. The three brothers came together in a back-pounding hug as the butler sighed and exited quietly. "You scare Hatch off every time. I swear, were it not for his devotion to my wife, he would hand in his notice. Where have you two been?"

Zachary glanced from the direction Devon came.

"Don't worry. You have perhaps thirty seconds before Anne appears and yells at you. Was it the weather that delayed you?"

Derek shook his head. "Anne would never yell at us. She adores us, or at least me."

Zachary shoved Derek a few inches. "She tolerates you. I finished up in Dublin five days ago, so I thought I'd meet up with Derek and travel north together."

Devon darted a look between his younger brothers. "And? Hurry, before Anne appears and—"

"Anne is already here." His wife glided into the foyer, her brow raised and her lips straight. Devon recognized her attempts not to smile. She opened her arms to her brothers-in-law, and they took turns enjoying her embrace before bestowing a kiss upon each cheek. "Where have you been, and what does Devon not want you to tell me?"

Zachary slipped an arm around Anne's waist and winked down at her. "Our sainted brother is worried we'll reveal agency secrets. Alas, our delay is not as interesting as that. Derek was in a dungeon."

Anne swatted Zachary. "Don't say such a thing."

"Uh, darling," Devon said. "I do believe he is serious."

Her gaze fell on Derek. "Whatever for?" Anne left Zachary's side and clasped Derek's arm. "What a horrid experience. Come, we'll call down to the kitchen for a hot meal, and Charles and Rhona brought a fine whisky with them."

Derek smiled at his brothers as he was led away.

Zachary leaned toward Devon and whispered, "Should we tell her I was not serious?"

"You could, but then you'd be lying, and we don't lie to my wife. What happened?"

Zachary shrugged. "Derek hasn't told me yet, though I gather it had something to do with the young lady of the house and a secluded cottage on the estate."

Devon's laugh echoed in the foyer, bringing Charles and Tristan to the entry.

"Finally made it." Charles shook Zachary's hand. "Derek's sharing quite a tale in there about a dark dungeon and a red-faced lord who swore to behead him."

Tristan gave Zachary a good slap on the shoulder. "It's almost as interesting as our ghost."

"Ghost?"

"Ah, yes." Devon put a hand on his brother's back and propelled him forward. "Rhona has a ghost, and we are trying to solve her murder."

They entered the parlor where everyone had gathered to sit or stand near Derek as he recounted his experience in the Yorkshire estate dungeon.

"For shame, Derek." Anne clucked her tongue like a mother would to a scolded child. Derek's grin said he knew she secretly enjoyed her brothers-in-law's antics.

"What's this about a ghost, Rhona?"

Long ago forgoing formal addresses among themselves, Rhona smiled at Zachary when he entered and addressed him in kind. "You should know better than now to believe anything your brother tells you."

"There's no ghost?" Derek asked.

"There is." Charles crossed the room to once more stand by his wife. "My wife has developed a knack for misstatements."

"What a pretty way to call a lie a lie," Alaina remarked.

"You cannot be surprised with as much time as we have spent around all of you." Anne caught the signal from the footman in the doorway. "Derek, Zachary, the kitchen has prepared a hot repast to tide you until the evening meal. It's served in the small dining room."

"Ever your servant, dear sister." Zachary bowed to Anne and waved to Derek. "Come along, brother, before they have us believing in ghost stories."

Derek kissed Anne's cheek as he passed and followed Zachary from the parlor.

Anne caught her husband's hand before he joined his brothers. "What did he mean, just then?"

"My brothers don't believe there's a ghost." Devon pressed a brief yet thorough kiss to his wife's lips. "We'll endeavor to convince them otherwise."

Devon had little luck convincing his brothers that a great former lady of the manor now haunted Greyson Hall, and likely had for over a century.

"It's not that we doubt your lovely wife, Charles, but we would have seen a ghost by now." Zachary, with his hunger now sated, leaned against the chair back.

"Agreed." Derek ate the last bite of his chicken, finished the water he preferred to wine, and added, "Though I did see a ghost myself once, so I can't discount the possibility."

Everyone shared a skeptical look before Tristan asked, "Where might this have been?"

"Three assignments back in Scotland. I was on my own that time and sent on a merry chase east of Inverness. Ended up in Culloden, and there—I'll swear it to my dying day— was a ghost on the battlefield."

"Or a man walking about," Charles said.

Derek shook his head. "No, I'm sure what I saw. Which means I've changed my mind. Charles, if your wife said she saw a ghost, it must be so."

"Well, I'd rather not see a ghost if it's all the same to

you." Zachary rose from the dining room chair. "But I don't mind joining the fun of the search."

"You might regret the offer." Devon also stood, and the others joined him. "As far as I can tell, it involves a lot of reading."

"Did you convince them?"

Devon kissed his wife's neck.

"Did you hear me?"

With a sigh, he rolled onto his back and lifted Anne until she rested on his chest. "I heard you and ignored the question."

"Rhona is quite serious about seeing this through, and Alaina and I will help her until we figure out why a ghost is haunting our house. Your brothers not once mentioned the ghost or helping us."

"I might have told them solving this mystery required a lot of reading." Devon kissed his wife's brow.

"The more help we all give, the more at ease Rhona will be." Anne scooted up his chest a little more until her mouth was a mere two inches from his. "Do you want Rhona unwell, so close to the birth of her first child?"

Devon rolled over, taking Anne with him and trapping her under his upper body. "You don't play fair, my dear."

Her lips curved. "Would you prefer I did?"

"Most definitely not." Before Devon returned to what he preferred to be doing with his wife, he lifted his head and searched the dark bedroom.

"I heard it, too." Anne tried to pull him back. "It is probably Lady Canterbury."

When Devon did not return her smile, Anne moved into a sitting position. "What do you hear?"

"Listen." Devon covered his wife with the blankets and roused himself from their bed. The voice grew louder, and this time the name it called for echoed from every corner of the room.

Hartley.

CHAPTER 12

Greyson Hall, Northumberland
December 21, 1782

The hallway carpet muffled each step. Silence and secrets surrounded her, and on this night, she would break through the spell of each and discover the truth behind Brice Maclean's visit to Greyson Hall.

Her husband had not joined her in their rooms since Brice made the assurance. Engaged in important matters was her husband's excuse, but what were those matters? And what did Brice Maclean, Alexander, and the others contribute to her husband's schemes? Spencer Canterbury was not a mysterious man, yet a man prone to secrets. She never cared about his goings-on before the Highlander reignited her desire to be gone from Greyson Hall, Northumberland, and England if she could manage it.

The skirt of her pale-blue, satin robe over a single petticoat swished about her legs as she stepped gently down the hall, her soft-soled slippers making nary a sound. She forewent a corset beneath the fitted bodice, relying only on her chemise for modesty, but at least she could breathe.

Grace tread lightly down the side staircase, used only by the highest level of servants during daylight hours, to avoid a late-night encounter with a guest or her husband.

Candles flickered in sconces along the walls to light the way, and a poor hall boy would be tasked with snuffing them when the last person went in search of their bed. Grace heard muffled voices before she rounded the corner and glimpsed shadows passing by the closed door to Spencer's study. Curiosity encouraged her closer; the sudden raised voice compelled her to stop.

"I'll not do it."

Whose voice? Not Brice's or her husband's. Alexander's, perhaps, or Whitford's or Bowley's? Their visit was as mysterious as the Highlander's.

"You will do it, or all our careful planning will be for naught."

Spencer Canterbury's voice carried a promise behind his stern warning.

"Aye, and what happens when your brother is found out?" Brice Maclean's voice was as clear to her as her own. His Scottish heritage became stronger and thicker as he spoke to her husband. "Alexander had no place to speak on our behalf."

A fist slammed on a desk, no doubt Spencer's. "He is my brother and has every right, for he did so at my behest. His actions—my commands—have made all of you wealthy men."

"No. No, I cannot be a part of this any longer."

"You have no choice, Whitford. We all know the consequences of backing away from the agreement."

A shiver surged through Grace at her husband's threat to

the man. My God, what have they done? Grace held a palm over her mouth to catch her sudden ragged breaths, and she backed away a few steps until she reached the corner and concealment. Moments later, the study door opened, and the steps of a single man strode in the opposite direction from where she hid.

"He won't be a problem." She heard Brice's voice clearly. They failed to shut the door after Whitford's retreat. "He has too much to lose."

"Yes, don't we all." Her husband's words lacked concern, which sent another shudder through her body. What did he have to lose? She thought of her son and again of Brice's admonition that she depart Greyson Hall. But to go where? Did he not realize the law did not allow her something so simple as freedom? That she would not leave her son behind, a son who, except by birth and love, did not legally belong to her?

"I won't allow it!" Spencer's shout dragged her from the incessant questions cluttering her thoughts. "I began this enterprise, and it continues by my word alone."

"Did you not say the money is nearly gone?" Brice asked. "That is why I am here, is it not? Because you need more?" Brice's voice deepened, and Grace strained to hear what came next. "Your commands mean nothing to me, Lord Canterbury. I agreed to this on my terms, and you accepted. If you no longer want my patronage, I will leave now."

So quiet did the hall become that Grace once more heard her breaths and covered her mouth. She pressed herself against the wall and laid a hand over her stomach to stop the trembling. *Her* money nearly gone? Fifty thousand pounds should have lasted long beyond their lifetime.

"Very well, Maclean, but I want Alexander to go with you."

"Brother, that's—"

"Quiet, Alexander! Maclean, what say you?"

"Acceptable."

Not a second's hesitation. Where is he going? And why did Spencer insist his brother go along?

"It's done then," Spencer said.

Footsteps entered the hall. To move now would draw notice, so Grace stayed around the corner, against the wall, and prayed they all went in the opposite direction. She heard their footfalls fade and released first the hand over her stomach, then the one over her mouth, until another took its place.

Grace clawed at the powerful grip and kicked against the large body pressing against her. Too tall to be her husband's. Too tall to be Alexander's. Unburdened now of fear, her eyes fluttered open and stared into angry green depths.

"'Tis me." Brice ground the words out, soft yet fierce. "By God, woman, you'll get yourself killed." He lowered his hand and remained close. "What has gone through your mind to be so foolish?"

"Will you betray me again?"

His head jerked back as though slapped by an invisible force. "Your question is as foolish as your actions."

"Then answer me this: Why are you at Greyson Hall?"

Brice rested his brow against hers before dragging her deeper down the hall to the side staircase. The door to the stairway clicked softly closed, entrenching them in darkness as black as soot. "You have no fear of me."

"You are wrong. I fear everything you do to me. The wanting and hope your mere presence promises."

"I will never harm you, Grace."

The shiver this time came from a place of longing. "I know."

"I cannot tell you why I am here."

"But you are leaving, are you not?"

Brice rested his hands at her waist. "You heard too much. Aye, I'm leaving after Christmas."

"With Alexander."

"Will you trust me, Grace? Trust me enough not to ask what I cannot tell you. Trust me enough to do as I say and ignore what I may do?"

She clutched the lapels of his dinner coat. "You ask too much."

"Yes." He brushed his lips over her cheek. "Will you trust me?"

"My son."

"He is safe for now."

To give her faith and her future to a man she barely knew defied the bounds of reasoning. "I will trust you. I *do* trust you. Give me the same confidence."

Rather than answer, he captured her mouth with his, and together, they spiraled into another existence shielded from hate, fear, and all that threatened the possibilities his kiss promised.

Reality returned, and their lips parted, yet his promise remained between them.

"Quit this place, Grace, please. Take your son and leave."

"Is the money truly almost gone?"

Brice's hands moved down her arms to clasp her hands. "I cannot tell you why, but I believe it is."

"And you are giving him some of yours to finance whatever scheme will no doubt get you killed."

He framed her face. "I have only just found you, Grace. Not even death will keep us apart, but I'll not be dying on you."

She knew no one could keep such a guarantee, yet she accepted the truth in his promise. "I have money of my own —a few thousand pounds. It will be enough to leave." The sympathy in his eyes told her another truth. "It is gone as well?"

"Nearly." Brice kissed her again and pressed a finger to her lips when a sound above drew their attention. After the count of thirty-seven seconds, he held her close. "You need to return to your rooms. Your husband will be occupied elsewhere."

"He often is." Grace peered up at him. "But how do you know?"

Brice brushed the pad of his thumb over her lips. "It does not matter. Do you know who it is?"

"Someone in the village, I should think. The women under this roof are too old or too loyal to me."

Brice quieted once more when a door opened and closed, a heavier door leading outside. Her husband had left the house without wondering where she'd been, if he'd bothered to look.

"His obsession with me is neither a secret nor a truth I wear proudly or vainly. It is not a village woman, is it?"

"Think of him no more tonight."

"Tell me!" She closed her eyes and counted until she calmed. "Please, tell me."

"It is not a woman, nor is it a dalliance. His obsession with you reaches far beyond the walls of this house." Brice brushed his lips over hers. "And he'll not have you again, Grace. I cannot tell you more, not yet. All I have is now yours."

"You do not know me."

His large hands framed her face once more. "I have known you almost always." Brice did not explain his cryptic response before adding, "After I leave, I'll make arrangements for you and your son."

"To go where?"

"Scotland."

CHAPTER 13

Greyson Hall, Northumberland
December 22, 1892

A hearty breakfast of eggs, mutton, bacon, toast, buns, and berries from the greenhouse filled an array of silver serving dishes across the sideboard. Rhona scanned the offerings and wanted to turn away almost as much as she wanted a sampling of everything.

She gently caressed her unborn child. "You'll have me waddling with your cravings, dear one."

Once Rhona was seated at the table, Charles leaned down and whispered, "You are as beautiful as you've ever been."

"You say that every morning." Still, she accepted his kiss.

"One of everything?"

"Except the mutton."

Charles smiled and went to the sideboard to fill a plate

for his wife. Devon and Anne were next to arrive, followed by Zachary and Devon.

Rhona asked, "Are Tristan and Alaina with the children?"

"They were going into the nursery when we came down." Anne joined Rhona when her husband took the plate from her hands to fill himself. "Did you hear anything last night? It would have been rather late."

Anne had spoken her question softly, so Rhona matched her whisper. "Not much can wake me from a deep sleep these days. What did you hear?"

Anne leaned a little closer. "I swear it was a woman calling out, and I am certain it was your ghost."

Devon set a plate with moderate portions in front of his wife. "I would suggest you not encourage my wife, Rhona, but I also heard the voice."

Anne peered up at her husband. "How did you hear what I just said?"

He whispered, "I hear everything." He kissed her before taking his own seat.

Anne scoffed and turned to Rhona again. "The woman called out for Hartley. That was Lady Canterbury's son, if I recall from the journal."

Rhona did not look at Charles when he placed her food on the table. "Yes, his name was Hartley. You are certain of what you heard?"

"My sanity is not in question because, as Devon confirmed, he also heard it."

Zachary and Derek sat across from their brother. Derek tucked into his food first while Zachary asked, "Have you found any other records of this Lady Canterbury?"

"Or descendants?" Derek asked after he swallowed a piece of bread. "They may have answers."

"As it happens, one of the Canterbury descendants lives

in this house. She's currently acting as a nanny." Anne spread jam on one half of a blaa bun. "Iris Gorran is her name; we've spoken with her and her mother. Her father is one of our tenant farmers."

"Do they resent you living here instead of them?" Everyone looked at Derek, who shrugged. "It is a valid question. When investigating any case, it is prudent to look at who benefits the most."

Devon smiled and shook his head at Derek. "You're not wrong, but get your head out of agency work for the holidays, if you will. We are not after solving a murder—"

"Or we are."

Now everyone at the table turned to Rhona. "Well, why else would she haunt this hall, and only at Christmas? Spirits only linger when there is a death under tragic circumstances or unfinished business, do they not? We must discover what happened to her before Christmas day."

Charles slid a hand over his wife's knee, and was rewarded with a kick from their child against his forearm. "We will help her."

"You won't believe what we discovered this morning." Alaina swept into the room alongside Tristan.

"She doesn't get all the credit, no matter what she tells you." Tristan pulled out a chair for his wife. "Tell them while I fix our plates."

Before Tristan reached the sideboard, Alaina turned to the others in excitement. "We found another journal. Not a personal journal, like Lady Canterbury's, but a record book of the estate."

Devon's brow raised, and he leaned a forearm on the table. "Where was this? I've not come across a record book yet."

"We could not sleep last night—"

Tristan cleared his throat.

"*I* could not sleep last night. The wind was fierce outside and kept me awake. My mind wandered to our ghost, so Tristan was kind enough to return to the study this morning."

Tristan sat next to his wife, set both their plates on the table, and stared at her.

"Very well. He was kind enough to let me drag him from our warm bed to search the study."

Tristan nodded once, thanked the footman who served them each tea, and said to the room, "I did not hear the wind and was sleeping quite well."

"Odd. I did not think the wind was strong last night," Charles said.

"It wasn't." Zachary ate the last bite of egg and leaned back. "I opened a window in my room for a bit of air, and not a whisper of a breeze."

"Well, I heard something. No matter, because we discovered the record book, and there is a mention of a Lady Canterbury attending a Christmas celebration in the village."

"What year?" Rhona asked.

"1782." Alaina glanced at Tristan for confirmation, who affirmed with another nod. "The journal is in your study, Devon, on the desk. If nothing else, it will give you more of a history on the estate."

"Then back to the study we go after breakfast." Devon finished the bun his wife left on her plate. "As Rhona has pointed out, we have only a few days until Christmas. We've accomplished more with less time."

Two hours later, the burning optimism reached during breakfast had dwindled to a cinder. From the chair behind Devon's desk, Rhona raised her head and rubbed the stiffness from her neck before Charles's hands took the place of hers. "There is nothing else in these records except for general estate affairs. Dates, rents, births and deaths of tenants, and so on. The wedding, their son's birth and christening, harvest celebrations, and two house parties are mentioned, but it seems the Canterburys rarely entertained."

"Not much luck over here, either." Devon lifted a stack of papers off a small table he shared with Anne. "It does not appear this estate has had a proper secretary since its inception, even under my uncle."

"You have yet to find one, either." Anne tapped three neat stacks of papers she'd created. "These are the ones just from your uncle's time here."

Devon pointed to the stacks. "All of that?"

"Didn't realize what you were getting into when you kept the place, did you?" Charles grinned. "I had much the same sentiment when I first inherited Blackwood Crossing."

"But you and Tristan were groomed to inherit your titles and estates. It's not at all the same." Devon sat back and sighed. "And I've no regret. We have come to love living here, but all this has made me realize I cannot carry on without help."

"The land agent at Claiborne Manor has been training his nephew in the trade." Tristan slid yet another book back into its place on the shelf. He and Alaina had removed and searched five rows of volumes, and his greatest discovery was that someone appreciated philosophical literature from different centuries and had an affinity for the law. "The young man is smart and eager, and his uncle is trustworthy, which bodes well for his nephew. If you're interested, I will inquire with his uncle."

"How young?" Devon asked.

"Young enough to not put on airs, but not so naïve that he'll run away at first sight of this room's disarray or the size of the estate. Twenty-two, I believe."

"Yes, please inquire. We'll give him a trial if he is interested in living in the cold north. Anything at this point

to save me from endless interviews and more of this." Devon
stood and stretched his back. "I'm going for a ride and will
meet up with my brothers if they've finished their business in
the village."

Anne added one more paper to the last stack. "They
never said why they went."

"To see a parish priest." Devon held up his hands to
ward off more questions. "That is all they said," Devon
spoke softly to his wife, bringing a smile to her mouth before
he quit the room.

"I'm going to look in on the children." Alaina rubbed a
little dust from her hands. "After I wash up a bit."

"I'll join you." Tristan removed a copy of *The Mysteries of
Udolpho* from the shelf, tucked it under his arm, and left the
room with his wife.

Anne crossed the room to the desk. "We will not solve the
mystery of your ghost in this study, Rhona."

With a deep sigh, Rhona rose from the seat with Charles
steadying her. "You are right, I fear. How else to find the
truth of her death, of her life? How can a noblewoman of
wealth and favorable circumstances simply disappear? We
have found no record of her death. What about the
Canterbury family did history feel they needed to hide?"

"Perhaps that is the question to answer."

Rhona contemplated her husband's comment while she
and Anne waited for him to explain.

"What if it is not her death that keeps her here but a
circumstance of her life? Rhona, you said a tragic death or
unresolved issues keeps a spirit anchored here. Anne, you
also grew up on ghosts and legends. Do you agree?"

Anne nodded. "Certainly. To my knowledge, the
caretaker's cottage on our property back in Ireland is still
haunted, as is the church."

"Interesting. All right, let's forget for the moment how

she might have died and try to learn more about how she lived."

"Then it is back to the journal."

Anne squeezed Rhona's hand. "No one knows better how she lived than Lady Grace Canterbury herself."

Devon puffed out warm breaths, only to watch each one create a small cloud in the frigid air. "This is not where I expected to find you." With reins in hand, he dismounted and took a circuitous route around three frost-covered graves to stand next to Derek in front of one that bore only three letters: LGC.

"Anne and I came to this graveyard once for the funeral of a tenant's grandfather. There is a cemetery next to the church, but those who have lived here longest prefer this plot." Devon peered at the landscape . . . land he appreciated for the memories he and Anne shared here, from their first moments of love to plans for their future family. Snow-covered hills and open land rolled into woodland beyond the farms, and where the sun and wind contrived to clear away snow, patches of brown grass yearned for spring. "Where is Zachary?"

"Still in the village. There's a wager on the books in the pub about the first Clayton heir, and he is taking advantage."

Devon's laughter caught his brother unawares in the somber setting. "Don't let Anne hear about it."

"She'll find it amusing," Derek predicted.

"Yes, and she'll ask one of you to place a wager for her."

Derek glanced sideways at his brother. "Is there anything you haven't told us?"

Devon slapped his brother's shoulder. "In good time. Why did you stop here?"

"Compelled to." Derek leaned forward to brush snow from the top of the headstone. "It must be her, Lady Grace Canterbury. Why hide her here?"

"If it is her, that is another question in the mystery of our lady ghost." Devon removed his soft wool cap long enough to rub a gloved hand over his hair and let the gentle breeze cool his brow. "What did you learn from the parish priest? He's been here less than three months."

"It's not him we went to see. The priest before him is the great-grandson of the vicar who lived here during the Canterbury's day, and he lives outside the village."

"How did you know about him?"

Derek smiled at his brother. "Zachary and I do not have your diversions, so when we are here, we spend time in the village with the people. They talk—a lot."

Devon almost grimaced. "I know you both exercise discretion, but if Anne learns that you—"

"We don't dally with any of the village girls if that worries you."

The rosy hue on Devon's face was no longer from the cold alone. "None of my business, though Anne will be happy to hear it."

"You talk about that sort of thing with your wife?"

Derek's incredulous expression drew a chuckle from Devon. "You should know by now I discuss everything with Anne—almost everything. Other than her desire to see you both as deliriously happy as we are, we do not discuss your personal assignations with the fairer sex."

"Ask one question," Derek mumbled. "As to what I learned from the priest, not much. However, his family has kept private records since before his great-grandfather's time."

Devon rounded on his brother. "Records from before the church burned?"

Derek patted the leather satchel hanging over his shoulder and across his chest. "Wrapped in soft leather to preserve them. I borrowed only the book from the years the Canterbury's lived, and I am sworn to return them in the condition I have borrowed them. I staked your life on it."

"My life?"

"Mine is worth far more than a sheath of papers."

Devon dropped an arm over his brother's shoulders. "I will give you the honor of repeating that to Anne. Come, let us find our wandering brother and return home. Our friends will be eager to read whatever is in those papers."

"I took a quick look while I was at the priest's cottage."

Humor now dampened—a reaction to Derek's sedate tone—Devon prodded his brother to continue.

"There is no record of Lady Canterbury's death at Greyson Hall."

"Or if she died there," Devon countered, "someone didn't want anyone else to know."

CHAPTER 14

Greyson Hall, Northumberland
December 21, 1782

N ails clawed over her skin, tearing flesh from her arms. A force wrenched her legs until she lay across the foot of the bed with her feet no longer held up by the down mattress. Under the weight of her struggle, the wool straps securing the mattress scraped across the bed frame.

"No!"

The exclamation caught in her throat, but she heard it in her mind, over and over. Grace kicked and met what felt like a wall, and each time the wall shoved her backward. Her eyes refused to compute anything except darkness, a veil of black between her and what she longed to see.

"No!"

"Grace!"

The next scream died against a firm hand. "'Tis me. Brice." The hoarse whisper penetrated her nightmare.

Shuddering breaths wracked her lungs, and sobs escaped between each one. Her sight now restored, she clung to Brice's chest, pulling him closer until nothing separated them. His arms surrounded her torso, and he pulled her legs between his. He covered her bare legs.

"It was not real." She buried her face against his shoulder, refusing to look up. Wait, bare legs. Grace opened her eyes then and rested her cheek against his chest so she could see some of her surroundings. Paintings rested on the floor against empty walls. The only light flickered from a single lamp near to where they were sitting . . . on a hard floor, not a down mattress.

"Where are we?"

"The attics."

His strangled voice whispered the answer. Grace finally looked up at him.

"How?"

"Do not think of it now. We need to get you cleaned up before—"

"Clean?" Grace leaned back against his arms enough to peer at herself. Her legs were indeed without stockings, though she still wore the rest of her clothes. The stench hit her next, a smell she recognized enough to know death lingered somewhere close. "Brice?"

"Do not look, Grace." Brice blocked the rest of the room with his large body as he knelt then stood, bringing her up with him.

"Move, now."

He did, though he kept his arms around her, and she kept an intense hold on him. The man lay across the room with his back toward them and his legs twisted. His head rested at an unnatural angle, and when it dawned on Grace why, she shuddered again and clutched her stomach. "He is dead." She raised her eyes to Brice's.

Brice tilted her chin up. "It is less than what he deserved."

"It was real. But he did not, there was not time . . ."

"No, he did not," Brice told her in answer to the question she could not finish. He lifted her into his arms and carried her so she could not clearly see the body when they passed. Neither of them spoke as he bore her close all the way to the suite she shared with her husband. "Lord Canterbury has not returned. You are safe here."

She sat quietly on the chaise while Brice removed her blue robe and petticoat. He left the chemise in place, unwound the plaid from around his own body, and wrapped her in the soft wool. "I do not remember how I came to be in the attics. Who was he?"

Brice poured water from a pitcher into a porcelain bowl, found a clean linen on the dressing table, and returned to her side. "Baron Whitford." With extraordinary care for such a strong man, he wiped her face with gentle strokes before dipping the linen again in water and repeating the process on each arm. The water became murky with dust and blood.

"What happened?"

"How you came to be there, I do not know."

She rested a palm against his face. "How did you come to be there?"

He stilled and allowed her to caress his rough skin with her smooth hand before he moved away. Brice remained silent while he opened a window and emptied the water. A current of bitterly cold air sneaked in before he secured the window. She waited as he stood, stared out through the glass, and waited still when he stepped back and closed the drapes.

"You are not here to help my husband or the others. What is it you must guard with such secrecy? You seek my trust yet offer none in return."

He circled and studied her. "You trust me."

Grace could not deny it. "Yes." She tightened the plaid around her shoulders, releasing his masculine scent from the fibers. "Our trust will strengthen or break based on what happens next."

"Will you go to Scotland?"

"Yes. No matter what happens, I will leave here and go wherever you send me for my sake and my son's. My trust in you runs deep enough. But what of thereafter?"

Brice crossed the room and knelt before her. "Forever."

Grace closed her eyes and leaned forward, resting her head on his shoulder. She desperately wanted to believe him. "Who is Baron Whitford to Lord Canterbury?"

He kissed her crown and brushed a long curl over her shoulder. "What he was no longer matters."

"My husband cannot know how he died." Panic overwhelmed her as all that transpired rose above her shock. "No one must know. We need to move him to—" When Grace tried to stand, she found herself held with gentle force on the chaise.

"The task falls on me alone." He framed her face. "Promise you will stay here and try to rest."

Grace shook her head. "I cannot sleep, not now."

He kissed her with urgency, then with care. "Promise me not to leave this room tonight."

Too overwhelmed to argue, she agreed. When Brice exited the room, Grace rubbed her cheek against the wool plaid and crossed to the window. She pulled back a drape and stared into the night until her legs trembled from exhaustion. Grace returned to the chaise, tucked her knees to her chest, and fought a bitter war with wakefulness before finally succumbing to sleep.

❄

The faint blue of early morning appeared over the snowy hills when Brice finished scrubbing Whitford's blood from his hands. He dispatched a message to London using his contact in the village, then returned to the attics, one level above the servants' quarters, hoping to learn why Whitford and Grace were there. Once the shock subsided, she would likely remember what happened. Until then, Brice needed answers. He scrubbed away what evidence he could of Whitford's death and unrolled a dusty rug over the remaining stain.

Morning light filtered through the window as Brice lifted a gilded cameo brooch etched in gold leaf off the floor. The one time he'd seen it was at Grace's throat in a portrait of her hanging in Lord Canterbury's study. He slipped the jewel into a pocket, spent another half hour searching, and left the attics without the needed answers.

On his way downstairs, he detoured to the nursery and stood at the door. The boy's nanny slept. Brice entered the room, not making a sound on the carpet, and approached Hartley Canterbury's crib. The boy bore his mother's coloring, mouth, nose, and soft alabaster hue of her skin. Brice saw little of his father in the angelic face.

He exited the room quietly and hurried to the bachelor's quarters and his own room. Brice ached to go to Grace, and for the first time since he affirmed his oath to his country, he wanted to tell someone everything about him. For six years, in pursuit of a better life and future for the Scottish people, he followed orders and kept his vow of secrecy. His oath weighed on him now as it never had before.

Brice rubbed both hands roughly over his face and watched out the window. He knew Lord Canterbury's path to and from the farm a quarter mile from the manor house, but he'd yet to snare the man. Twice now, he had followed Grace's husband, only to find the farm empty. He needed

more time to search the cottage and outbuildings, and had he
not returned early last night . . . why had Grace gone to the
attics? And why had Whitford followed her? He knew
Whitford's preferences shied away from the fairer sex, so
defilement had not been the baron's motive.

Lord Canterbury's approach matched the rising sun over
the hill where a small graveyard rested. The horse upon
which he sat carried him smoothly over the field, though the
man jostled and swayed in the saddle to the stable, where
Brice lost line of sight.

The rest of the house party would not be awake for
hours, which gave him time. Not a lot, but enough. As he
turned from the window, the corner of his eye caught a
flicker of movement. The long wool cloak trimmed in fur
could have belonged to any of the women present at
Greyson Hall. Except, even with the heavy fabric and hood
covering her flaxen hair, his mind and body recognized
Grace.

She sidled close to the manor's stone walls until she
reached the house's edge and Brice's vision. He waited and
watched as she returned to view, leaving the cover of the wall
for an open field. Brice swore, grabbed his wool coat, and
slipped into it while hurrying out of his room.

"Leaving so early?"

Brice stilled at Lord Canterbury's question. He spun on
his heel and smiled at his host. "Off for an early ride. My
horses are still resting from the journey here. I planned to
beg a mount from a groomsman, but now that you're here,
do you mind?"

Lord Canterbury waved away Brice's concern. "Not at
all." He raised a finger. "Before your ride, I will take
advantage of Whitford and Bowley's absence and request a
private audience with you."

"What of Alexander?"

"I will relay our conversation with him later. Will you join me in my study?"

The words formed a question, and the tone conveyed an order. Brice heard both and chose to yield to whatever game Canterbury was playing. He thought of Grace moving across the hills alone, though to follow her now would be to alert her husband. "I am at your disposal, my lord."

Canterbury led the way down the stairs to the study and closed the door once Brice entered. "I do not mistake you for a fool."

Brice nodded.

"You are aware of my absence last evening."

"I am."

"Good. I appreciate your honesty, Maclean. It is far too rare a quality among our kind." Canterbury walked around to his desk and remained standing. His gaze drifted and fell on Grace's portrait across the room. "The news I have to disclose is most unpleasant for me. However, I fear we must escalate our plans."

"It is not impossible." Brice studied Grace's husband for any sign of what deception he was about to attempt. "However, to deviate now will be to alert the people we hope to avoid. Discretion and secrecy are crucial."

"I agree, but we have no choice." Canterbury sighed and leaned forward on his desk. "My brother has apprised me of a most disturbing incident involving my wife."

Discipline bested concern before it manifested on Brice's face. "Has Lady Canterbury learned of our dealings?"

"I fear she may have." Canterbury lowered himself into the high-backed chair and slumped against the thick padding. "Alexander witnessed her searching my study two nights ago. He feared telling me, but we have all vowed to protect the cause."

Brice knew it for a lie, yet his expression revealed nothing. "Did he approach her?"

Canterbury shook his head. "He would never dare. No, it regrettably falls to me to punish her, though I find I cannot commit such a sin. She must be brought to our side, or—"

"Or what?"

The edge to Brice's voice prompted closer scrutiny by Lord Canterbury. He leaned forward and tapped his finger pads on the desktop. "You have yourself said discretion and secrecy are vital."

Finally allowing his anger to surface, Brice approached the desk. "I dinna kill women. Ne'er will."

Canterbury pushed up on his hands and stood, leaning halfway over his desk. "You will do what must be done, as will we all."

"Aye, but no' that."

"I sometimes forget your lesser birth until you speak with that awful burr."

Brice smiled before putting his back to Lord Canterbury.

Canterbury's fist hit the desk. "We are not done!"

At the door, Brice said over his shoulder, "Aye, we are. 'Tis my money ye want, and ye'll no' be seeing another pence if ye dinna stop yer blathering." He returned to the desk and to using his perfected speech. "No woman, child, or innocent will be harmed for our cause. You knew well enough that was my condition. If it no longer suits you to keep your word, I will withdraw myself and my purse from Greyson Hall this morning."

"You will risk all we have sacrificed for one woman?"

Brice watched his arms raise and extend, and his hands reach for Canterbury's neck. Strong fingers encircled the narrow column of flesh, bone, and blood. He felt the tips of his fingers squeeze, pressing against the skin—

"Maclean!"

Brice emerged from his deadly fantasy and stared at the man who spoke too easily of his wife's death. He may be unwilling to kill her himself, but no doubt he'd find someone willing. Alexander came immediately to mind, and should the younger Canterbury get Grace in his clutches, he would do far worse than murder.

"If we must sacrifice our cause to spare an innocent life, then yes, I will risk it all."

CHAPTER 15

Greyson Hall, Northumberland
December 23, 1892

Derek tossed the church records aside, then bent down to pick them off the bedroom floor. Darkness had descended, dinner and friendship enjoyed, and more papers and journals read and discarded as useless before everyone retired to their rooms.

The only new mention of Lady Grace Canterbury was in reference to a Somerson Farm, which in the 1780s and '90s had been part of the estate left to ruin and finally torn down in 1805. A new farmhouse erected. The Somersons, according to the old priest, left Northumberland soon after for America. The inability to question them became yet another impediment in their search, though why Derek should now feel as invested as Rhona, he knew not.

He left the warmth of his bedroom in the family wing,

his destination the study where Devon kept his finest stock of whisky. Derek rarely imbibed—his life depended on remaining clear-headed—but tonight, sleep remained beyond his grasp, and a dram sometimes helped cloud his mind enough to allow rest. He might even drag Zachary from his bed for a round of cards. Derek withdrew his pocket watch, noted the hour of two o'clock in the morning, and decided against disturbing anyone else.

Still clothed in the trousers and shirt from dinner, he almost returned for his jacket when a chill raced over him, starting at his legs and rushing up and over his head. Derek seldom resorted to exaggerated thoughts, yet the face half a foot from his own was the most angelic, most gloriously beautiful face he'd ever encountered. Pale, golden hair framed her delicate features and curled to her waist. A small, perfect mouth parted slightly, and her wide eyes, more silver than blue, bore tremendous sadness . . . sorrow so deep, Derek rubbed a hand over his heart to dull the ache.

A single tear glistened down her luminescent cheek as she pointed down the hallway. Derek's gaze followed her direction, and he saw nothing except a dark and empty hall. "What is it you want us to find?" He did not expect her to answer. Neither did he expect, when he turned toward her again, to find her gone.

Devon and Anne were the only two at the breakfast table later in the morning when Devon entered the light-filled room. Winter's gloom blew away to leave the snow glistening. The glare off the windows proved more than Derek's eyes could handle, and he looked away.

"It will be a lovely day for a ride." Anne smiled up at him from her chair, then her smile faltered when she got a good look at him. "Did you sleep poorly?"

Ignoring the sideboard, Derek sat across from Devon and

Anne and accepted a cup of coffee from a footman. "Have you come across the original plans for the house, the first plans when Lord and Lady Canterbury lived here?"

Devon stopped eating, and Anne set down her teacup. They shared a look Derek deciphered as one of those that only the two people involved understood.

"We have not." Derek wiped a linen over his mouth. "It is unlikely they still exist. However, I understand that the current structure bears many similarities to the original."

"What of the hall where Zachary and I sleep in the family wing?"

"I imagine it was always bedrooms." Devon quieted when a footman entered with another hot-covered dish and arranged it on the sideboard before quietly leaving. "What is this about?"

"He has seen her." Anne's eyes gleamed. "You have seen the ghost, haven't you?"

"Early this morning."

Anne's head tilted slightly, and she leaned forward. "What did she do?"

"And what does it have to do with the family bedrooms?" Devon asked.

"She pointed." Derek shrugged and drank half his coffee, scalding his throat. He reached for the glass of water in front of him and swallowed deeply.

"She rattled you, more like." Devon looked up and waved in whoever stood at the threshold. "Where did she point?"

"Where did who point?" Charles led Rhona into the room with Zachary not far behind.

"Down the hall."

"What hall?" Anne asked.

"Who pointed what down which hall?" Zachary asked.

Derek wished he'd had the wherewithal after his ghostly encounter to make it to the study and consume Devon's entire liquor stock. Then he would still be asleep, possibly for the rest of the day. The idea suited him splendidly.

"Derek?"

Devon's voice dashed Derek's hopeful wish to be abed. "Lady Canterbury stared at me, raised her arm, and pointed down the corridor past my and Zachary's rooms. Then she vanished."

With a full plate of food, Zachary settled himself next to Derek. "Did you check the rooms down that way? There are five more." Zachary glanced at his brother. "Uncle Wynton left you a mausoleum, Devon. You'll need a dozen children if you hope to fill the rooms."

Praying for patience, Derek scowled at Zachary, then ignored him in favor of the others. "Yes, I looked. I checked each room except for the last one on the north side. I don't have the key."

Anne perked up. "Key? There are no locked doors in that hall." She peeked at her husband who confirmed.

"No, not a single locked door. In fact, except for when one of us locks a door from the inside, we keep no room in this house locked." Devon garnered the butler's attention from across the room. "Hatch, are you aware of any locked rooms in the family's wing?"

The older man gave a slow shake of his head. "No, sir, not a one. I shall, with your permission, sir, handle the matter."

"No need to bother yourself with it, Hatch. I'll go up shortly."

"Curious," Rhona said, "that the spirit should know of a locked room when you do not, Devon. Who would have a key?"

"There are two master keys to unlock every room," Anne

said. "Hatch has one, and we keep the other. The housekeeper cares for the individual keys on an enormous brass ring she keeps in her office sitting room."

Rhona peered around her husband. "What else did the spirit do, Derek?"

"She cried a single tear. I have never seen such sadness."

Zachary swallowed a piece of sausage and grinned at his brother. "Sounds more like you fell in love."

"Love?" Derek shook the thought away. "No, though I won't deny that something about her pulled at me."

"It is the same for me." Rhona's whisper gained everyone's attention. "I cannot explain how she touched me and make sense of it. We have to help her find peace, and yet there is little time left. If we fail, must she wait another year in this prison?"

Derek held Rhona's gaze. "We won't fail."

"Won't fail what?" Tristan and Alaina walked into the breakfast room, each carrying a child.

"We won't fail Lady Canterbury." Anne rose and held out her arms for baby Ambrose. "We have not seen enough of them, always tucked away in the nursery." Alaina obliged by rounding the table and handing her younger son into Anne's arms.

"That is because when they leave the nursery, they somehow multiply, and one must grow another pair of arms." Alaina subtly rubbed her forearms. "Having children at the table is not the done thing."

"You know we love to have them around. Besides, if we were to follow convention, we ladies would break our morning fast in bed. A decidedly dull practice." Anne cooed at Ambrose and tweaked his little nose.

Devon whispered for her hearing only, "Only dull when you are abed alone, my dear."

Anne swatted her husband's arm, then softened it with a

smile before giving her attention to Alaina again. "The housekeeper informed us earlier that Iris is helping her mother deliver bread about the estate. This is her usual half day."

"Iris offered to stay, but we have already inconvenienced her enough."

"Iris!" Christopher clapped his hands and bounced once in his father's lap.

"Yes, you quite adore her." Alaina kissed her son's nose, and now that her arms were free from Ambrose's weight, she ushered her husband to remain sitting while she prepared a small plate for young Christopher and a scoop of porridge for Ambrose. Without asking, Hatch relieved her of the dishes and carried them to the table for her.

They all knew better than to dress down the butler . . . or any butler. They were among the most intimidating of men. When Alaina sat, Tristan settled their son in the high chair a footman produced and moved the small portioned plate to the tray table. "Thank you, Hatch, you do think of everything."

The butler nodded, and Alaina stared at each person at the table. "What were you discussing when we entered?"

A headache spread to Derek's temple. "If I may have use of your key, brother, I believe I will inspect the locked room."

Without making a sound, Hatch appeared at Derek's side, his palm open, the key laying in its center. "You are terrifying, Hatch."

The butler nodded. "Thank you, sir."

Derek's headache eased a fraction. "I will use it with the utmost care." Not waiting for a response, Derek exited the breakfast room, traversed the great hall, and bounded up the main staircase. By the time he reached the last door beyond the family's bedrooms, Zachary had caught up with him.

"She must be special."

Derek slid the key into the hole, turned, and heard the click. "We help people, Zachary, and that is what I am doing."

"People, not ghosts." Zachary followed him into the room and shivered at the temperature drop. "Devon mentioned something about a room having a draft. Is this the same one?"

"No, that was the original nursery." To Derek, the space resembled most of the bedrooms, albeit slightly smaller, with its luxurious furnishings, ornate paintings, and expensive linens, all remaining from their Uncle Wynton's brief time in the house. Anne had only the primary rooms refreshed, giving the drawing room, parlor, morning room, the library, and her and Devon's bedroom a few more feminine touches. Otherwise, Uncle Wynton's taste had run to the opulent, with little variety.

A dark rosewood bed, with carved headboard and footboard, filled most of the room. Matching tables graced either side of the bed. One was empty, while upon the other rested an oil lamp and a single leather-bound book.

"There's no dust."

"Not a speck, which begs the question, 'Why lock it?'"

"Perhaps it was your ghost."

Derek leveled a glare at his brother. "Are you here to help or annoy me?"

"I am quite adept at accomplishing both at once." Zachary stood with his back along the wall opposite the bed and waved his arms above his head.

"What are you doing?"

"Looking for the draft. Ah!" Zachary turned and tapped the wall next to the hearth. "It's here."

Derek nudged his brother aside and trailed his fingers

along the paneling. It gave a quarter inch. "Come and help me give it a push." The brothers braced their shoulders against the panel. On the first try, it barely moved. With more effort, the panel slid in and to the left to hide behind the wall. "This is not the answer I had hoped to find."

There wasn't enough room for them both to stand at the narrow doorway, so Zachary looked over Derek's shoulder and shuddered. "Devon needs to see this room."

Derek ducked his head to enter, though once inside the small space, there was a foot of space between him and the board ceiling. He breathed in and immediately coughed against the inhale of dust. Derek crossed the room and worked the frame of the single tiny window until the wood gave and it slid open. "Uncle Wynton did not build this room." A narrow cot in a brass frame rested against one wall. Next to the bed, a small table was covered in several loose and weathered pages. An old oil lamp with a cracked chimney lay turned over next to the papers. When some of the dust cleared the air, Derek spotted the thick cloth covering what appeared to be the shape of a frame.

Zachary reached it first, and removing it carefully to avoid releasing too much dust from the cloth, he dropped the fabric next to the painting it had revealed. "My God."

Derek approached the painting slowly and with reverence. When he stood a foot away, all tension left his body and ceased movement. Overcome with a need to touch the face in the portrait, Derek caressed the fair skin of her cheek with a single finger. "It is her."

His jaw no longer slack, Zachary asked, "This is the ghost?"

"She is." He trailed his finger once over her mouth before stepping back. Derek's words reached only a whisper. "Tell Devon."

Zachary stared a few moments longer, released a deep

breath, and left the small room. Derek knew not how long he stood alone gazing upon Grace Canterbury's likeness. She wore the softest of smiles, leading him to believe she'd been engulfed with love, for no other emotion etched such serenity and peace upon a visage.

"Derek?"

Only Devon entered the space, though Derek heard other voices in the bedroom behind him. "Zachary told us what you . . . found." His eyes had alighted upon the portrait. "And that is her? You're certain?"

Derek nodded. "It's unhealthy for Rhona to come in here, so my word will have to suffice."

"Charles has already threatened to lock her away if she attempts to join us. As it happens, she is with Alaina and the children in the drawing room." Derek bent forward to scrutinize the painting. "She was magnificent."

Derek heard the admiration in his brother's voice, but it lacked the awe Derek felt. "She was." With gentleness, he lifted the painting and followed his brother from the room. Tristan pushed aside the drapes, and sunlight flooded the room. Derek rested the image against the bed's footboard so everyone could view it.

"Now I understand your determination to help, Derek." Charles squatted down and leaned within a few inches of the portrait. "It appears unsigned. The skill and talent remind me of George Romney's work, but the woman's expression the artist captured is quite extraordinary. Rhona will want to see this."

Anne studied the hidden room now, momentarily ignoring the painting. "Is it possible the builders never saw this room during refurbishment? It does not appear to have been touched in ages."

"If so, Uncle Wynton was ignorant of the room's

presence here. He would not have kept it, nor allowed such a gem as this art to be hidden away."

"Why," Tristan began, "would our lady ghost lead Derek to this discovery?"

Devon lifted the painting. "That is an excellent question."

CHAPTER 16

Greyson Hall, Northumberland
December 22, 1782

H er lungs burned; her skin prickled. She had not prepared herself for the frigid temperature drop or the moisture creating a layer of frost on her heavy wool cloak. The fur lining kept most of the chill away so long as she held the edges close to her body.

Grace peered upward from beneath the cloak's hood. Sunlight continued to beat upon the estate through downy clouds moving across the sky, though it offered no warmth. Her leather boots failed to prevent the snow's invasion from dampening her stockings, and still, they carried her over the last hill where she spied her destination.

A few minutes later, she leaned against the stone vault, bracing her body as she slowed her breathing. Any of the guests under Greyson Hall's roof could have slipped the carefully penned note beneath her bedroom door.

. . .

YOUR FATE IS IN MY HANDS. I KNOW WHAT HAPPENED
IN THE ATTICS AND WILL AWAIT YOU AT THE
MAUSOLEUM.

She had memorized the note before tossing it into the hearth
and waited while the paper curled and the flames consumed.
Grace still could not recall what transpired in the attic or
how she came to wear a dead man's blood. The only
memory she refused to release was of Brice carrying her
from the dusty room and washing the evidence from her
skin. She knew he had returned to the attics to discard the
evidence of Baron Whitford's death and her possible
involvement.

If she had killed him with her own hand, she would
remember. Grace held fast to that sliver of conviction.

On a bracing breath, Grace urged the thick, oak door to
the vault open. It creaked but gave way with less effort than
she expected. Whoever sent the note waited within. She
cursed herself for a fool and almost retreated. The quiet
laugh, however, stalled her departure.

"Who is there?"

Alexander loomed from a shadowy corner beyond two
stone coffins. "Did you think yourself safe?"

Grace refused to enter. The cold outside was nothing
compared to Alexander's lecherous examination of her
person. He could see far more with the light behind her.
"What do you hope to accomplish, Alexander? Your brother
will despise you."

His carnal gaze continued with each step he took
forward. "My brother is no longer the besotted swain you

believe him to be." Alexander skimmed a hand over a coffin. "He has learned the truth of your treachery, and dear Grace, he will not risk all he's worked for, not even for you."

"You speak in lies. If treason has been done, it is not by my actions."

Alexander shrugged. "My brother believes differently."

Grace reversed a step.

"There is nowhere to run and no one to save you this time, dear sister." Alexander paused at the base of the coffins and crossed his arms. "You would do better to court my favor rather than my ire. This," he waved a hand in front of him, "will be less painful with your acceptance."

"You claimed to know something about the attics."

"Let us not play games, Grace. Neither of us cares what happened there."

"I awakened with a dead man near me. How could you possibly know anything?"

His lewd smile widened. "Who did you suspect silenced Whitford? He was a threat, and my brother always cautioned me to deal with threats most industriously."

"A threat to whom?"

Alexander made a quiet clicking sound with his tongue. "You have not earned that knowledge. True, it would have been better if a servant had found you there with Whitford. The Highlander has proven more resourceful than I expected, and he keeps getting in my way." He shrugged, then stood straighter and advanced once more. "Not this time, though. Enough talk, Grace. Come here."

The ray of sunlight shining into the vault brightened and momentarily blinded Alexander. Grace retreated one more step but not before Alexander's arm snaked out to grab an edge of her cloak and yank her toward him.

"No, Grace. Your Highlander cannot save you this time."

A tear fell down her reddened cheek. "He will not have

to." The blade sliced cleanly into Alexander's gut. His eyes widened, and his lips moved, though no words emerged, only gasps and gurgles.

Grace was vaguely aware of shouting from outside the vault and the ringing in her head that prevented those shouts from making sense.

Brice pulled her away from Alexander and pressed her behind him. "Take my horse and go, Grace. Now!"

She froze and stared at the bloody blade in her grasp. Grace uncurled her fingers and let it fall to the stone floor, where it landed with a sharp clank.

Brice hefted Alexander into his arms and deposited him on a coffin. Alexander fisted Brice's plaid and gurgled blood as it slowly pooled in his mouth. He tugged until Brice leaned over him. Grace was too far away—astonishment at her actions had paralyzed her next to the door—to hear the whisper, and then Alexander's life sputtered from his body.

"Brice." Grace's whisper of his name gained his notice. "I did not . . . I wanted . . ."

Seconds later, safe in the cradle of his arms, Grace wept. Not for the loss of Alexander's life but for the choice she felt had to be made and for the loss of innocence in carrying it out.

"Why Grace?" Brice spoke against her ear, and his fierce hold never slackened.

"He would have—"

"Why did you not tell me?" Brice leaned back to look at her. "Why did you come here alone?"

The truth, she decided, was best. "I did not think, not at the time, and I hoped whoever sent the note could give me answers." She focused her watery eyes on him. "I was right."

"Alexander killed Whitford?"

Grace nodded. "He said Baron Whitford was a threat but

did not expound on why, nor explain what any of it has to do with me."

"You came prepared," Brice said, his voice rough.

"Not to commit such a sin as I have done—never that. He would not have let me leave here alive."

"You did right." Brice brushed back the pale gold locks fallen from a loose twist about her head. "It is not over, Grace. You must leave England this very day—this moment."

"My son!"

"I have persuaded a maid to bring your son to the cottage behind the stable. You will leave from the village."

She grasped his plaid and clenched. "You are not coming with us?"

"Not yet." His lips pressed hard against hers. "Soon, but there is much still for me to do here."

"What of Alexander?"

Brice halted her attempt to peer around him. "It is not a sight you ever need gaze upon again. Come." He raised the hood over her hair and turned her to precede him from the mausoleum. "Stop here. Hold out your hands." Brice bent over, picked up a handful of snow, and rubbed them over every inch of her hands. He repeated the process twice before all evidence of blood was removed.

"It has been a day for death," she whispered.

"Not yours, and that is what you must cling to now." Brice searched his pocket for the brooch he found in the attic, and finding it missing, unpinned a silver thistle from inside his plaid and used it to secure the cloak over her bodice. "Let us go and get your son."

"Wait. Spencer will wonder about his brother." She clutched his forearm. "Someone will find him there. The guests at the hall—"

"Are leaving. Your husband ordered them gone as I was

leaving. He'll not recover once word of his hospitality spreads upon his peers. Neither will you."

"I care nothing for any of them."

Brice wrapped an arm around her shoulder and squeezed. "No one will find Alexander before it is time." Brice whistled, and a man on horseback appeared from around the mausoleum. "See it done, Murdo."

Grace studied the newcomer with more curiosity than perhaps the situation warranted. But how had he come to be there? Coarse red hair covered Murdo's head and splayed about his shoulders. The same red extended to the thick beard masking half his face. Murdo's Scots dialect was so thick she caught only a few of the words of his reply to Brice.

Brice gave her little opportunity to continue her study of the other man. He lifted her onto the back of a horse tied next to a lone rowan tree barren of its leaves, the silvery-gray bark catching glimmers of sunlight off the snow. Such simple beauty lightened and swept her thoughts from the blood speckles on her bodice for the barest of moments. She wanted to hold her son in her arms, to take him far away from the madness that was his father.

Murdo dismounted and entered the vault, saying nothing more to either of them. Brice swung up behind Grace and lifted her onto his lap so her legs hung over the side. He held her close. "No one will find Alexander."

She wondered about his assurance on the quick return to Greyson Hall. They stopped at the cottage behind the stable, where, to her bewilderment, the stable master waited within. She understood the cottage to house the man, and she had only seen him once, but why was he waiting for them?

Brice ushered her inside and led her to the hearth where a fire blazed. "Archie, we haven't much time."

Grace stared at the man who had been in her husband's employ for five months. "You know each other?"

Brice nodded. "Aye. He will not say a word to your husband. Archie, where is the bairn?"

Archie darted a glance briefly at Grace before answering Brice. "He's not come."

"Where is the maid, Nola?"

"I've not seen 'er."

Panic swelled Grace's heart and shook her voice. "Brice."

"I will find him." To Archie, he said, "Guard her with your life."

"Brice." She latched onto his hand. "Why has Spencer not come looking for me?"

He pressed a kiss to her brow. "Wait here with Archie. I'll not be long."

Brice hovered in the narrow servant's stairway until he heard footsteps walk past the door to the second level and fade down to the hallway. Nola had not been below stairs, and no imprints in the snow meant she, nor anyone else, had recently left by way of the servants' entrance.

When all was silent beyond the door, Brice accessed the hallway and went to the nursery. Once again, a lull greeted him. This time, the quiet sparked a series of bristle-like sensations to creep across his skin. The nursery was empty.

"Where is my wife?"

The door creaked and stopped a foot short of closing. Spencer Canterbury hovered behind it, remaining in the corner as he studied Brice.

"Safe."

Spencer pressed his lips tightly together and left the corner, though he kept a safe distance between him and Brice.

"Where is the boy?"

"You mean my son?" Spencer's brow raised. "Why should his whereabouts concern you? I have loyal servants, Mr. Maclean, and I daresay those who succumbed to your persuasions are no longer my concern."

Brice forced his imagination away from what Canterbury might have done to Nola.

"You should have killed me when the chance presented itself, Mr. Maclean."

"Aye, but dinna mistake a servant saving ye for loyalty, Canterbury. 'Tis all over."

"What is over? Our scheme, our plan for which we have all sacrificed so much?" Spencer slammed a fist into the wall, breaking through to the plaster and likely bruising his knuckles. "You are as guilty as I am of treason."

"Nay. 'Tis over, Canterbury, all of it."

Spencer's eyes narrowed. "I think we both speak in riddles. What do you believe is over?"

The distance closed by three feet with Brice the aggressor. He gained a modicum of satisfaction from seeing the other man back up a step. "Everything ye wanted. All ye sought tae gain. 'Tis over."

Spencer clenched and unclenched his fists. "Not if she ever wants to see her son again."

The words hit Brice like a fist to his face. "What have ye done with the bairn?"

"Bring her to me within the hour, or she will forever lose her son."

Considering himself safe to leave, Spencer skirted Brice with his back straightened by misplaced arrogance and a defeat he'd yet to win. Brice struck out his arm, the force of it stopping Spencer.

"If ye've done e'en a hair of harm to the boy, ye'll see the dark inside of a grave afore ye take yer last breath." A visible shudder coursed through Spencer. He did not yield, nor respond to the threat. "Where is he?"

"Out of my way, Highlander. You may join the other guests in leaving this house. Our agreement is voided."

Brice lowered his arm and leaned closer to Spencer. "No agreement ever existed."

A flush spread into Spencer's cheeks, and he shuffled a step closer to the exit. "You may improve your dialect, but you will still be a Scotsman without power and purpose."

"You mistake me, Lord Canterbury. No agreement existed because I was never part of your plan. It is over. Not in the way I had hoped, but over nonetheless."

Spencer frowned. "You are the one who speaks only in riddles."

"Where is the boy?"

"Gone."

Brice slammed Spencer against the door. "What do you mean gone?" Spencer struggled against the force of Brice's grip. "Where is he?"

"If I cannot have them both, she cannot have him!"

"No!" Grace appeared in the doorway and attacked her husband. Her nails clawed at his face, scoring the skin over one eye before Brice wrenched her away from Spencer. "He cannot!" She pushed at Brice's arm around her waist. "He cannot have him!"

Servants knew well enough not to disturb their employers, even amid a fight, but Brice harbored no doubt that fortune's favor would not last much longer. "Grace." He half carried her farther into the room while she kicked out, and a moment later, she collapsed, supported only by his strength. "Grace, look at me." He turned her in his arms. "Where is Archie?"

The shaking began in her head and hastened through her body. "Everyone is dying, Brice. Everyone is dying."

He lifted her hand and pressed it to her chest, over her heart, then over his. "Not everyone."

Spencer did not flee as Brice expected. He stood near the doorway, smiling.

"Do you want him back, Grace?"

Brice put himself firmly between Grace and her husband. "You won't get her."

Spencer ignored him. "Do you want to see your son again, Grace?"

Grace choked back a sob, braced herself against Brice as she steadied her legs, and glared at her husband. "What do you want, Spencer? My blood, my body, my money—or what you have not taken of it already? It is all yours, but you cannot have my son."

Brice blocked her from moving around him. "He'll have none of it."

"Brice." The desperate plea she could not put into words was in his spoken name.

"I cannot let you go with him, Grace."

"And I cannot lose my son." Her eyes glistened as she stared up at him. It was a look of love, hope, and a promise to return to him. "Forgive me."

Spencer growled and reached for her. Grace lunged backward into Brice's arms. "You will not lay a hand upon me, Spencer. Not until Hartley is returned to me."

"After that?"

She closed her eyes. "Then you will do what you must."

Brice still held her and growled out, "No, Grace."

This time she whispered in his ear. "Trust me. Please, trust me as I have trusted you."

Spencer walked from the room, expecting her to follow. Grace did not disappoint him.

CHAPTER 17

Greyson Hall, Northumberland
December 23, 1892

R hona sat next to the hearth in the parlor, the open journal in her lap.

Death has scarred my soul, and I make this record should my mind ever follow and prevent my recollections. I gained a promise from Brice this very day that all is not lost, and one day we shall find my most beloved. I feel his heartbeat as if it rested in my chest. Could such a sensation be possible if he no longer lived?

"She writes of her child." Rhona rested a palm over her unborn child and willed it to move. The baby within rewarded her silent prayer. It lived as Grace's son had lived. "How could she have lost her baby? What could have happened to him?"

"Read on, Rhona," Alaina urged.

"There is nothing more." Rhona closed the journal. "The remaining pages are blank. What she went through is unimaginable."

"Are you forgetting, love," Charles said, "what you went through to gain your freedom from your father? Or Alaina and Anne? What you both endured to find the truth about your pasts, your families, and what it took to be here in this moment together?" Charles removed the journal from Rhona's lap to a small end table. "You women too rarely give yourselves the credit your resilience deserves."

"Charles is right." Devon stood behind his wife's chair and stroked her cheek. "You still astound me."

"It is wonderful for you to say, but we three had all of you." Alaina held her husband's hand. "Without you . . . I cannot imagine."

Tristan brought Alaina's hand to his lips and kissed the soft skin. "And Grace had her Highlander."

"But what happened to them? We have found no other record to tell of what occurred next." Alaina caught Devon's attention. "Where is Derek? I believe Zachary is still in the village, but I expected Derek to want to hear this, considering what he found and his encounter with . . . Grace."

A silent agreement passed over the room that Grace could no longer be called a ghost or spirit. She possessed a name. Grace Canterbury had loved deeply and suffered greatly; most importantly, she had lived.

Devon bent over to kiss his wife's cheek. "I'll go in search of Derek. I already suspect where he might be." Five minutes later, Devon found his brother in the hidden room, sitting at the table and staring at the narrow, dust-covered cot. "Derek?"

His brother did not look up when he spoke. "What hell she suffered in here. At least it wasn't for long, but to wonder if she'd ever leave must have scarred her soul."

"What makes you believe she was not in here long?"

Derek laid a flat hand over the papers. Previously loose and scattered over the table, but now stacked, they lacked the dust of the other surfaces. His brother appeared oblivious to the cold room, growing colder by the minute from the still-open window.

"She wrote what amounts to three journal entries on these papers." Derek lifted one and read.

I never knew such a room existed under this roof, nor do I suspect Spencer expected me to learn of it. The bedroom is one of several we have never used in the family wing, and what a peculiar space. So sparse and sad. Crates line the wall opposite the window, and from the lack of markings in the dust on the surrounding floor, they have not been there long. How did they come to be here without my knowing?

It is time I waste putting these nonsensical thoughts to paper. The waiting is unbearable. Where is my son? Where is Brice? Has he found Hartley? Will my son live beyond this day? Does he even live now?

Spencer took the journal I carry with me always, so I use these papers and hope someday they are found. Unless Spencer plans to never release me. What then will come of my beloved son?

No, I must remember Brice. He will save me. I know it as I know the very heart beating in time with his, with my son's. Where are they?

"We'll have to prepare the women before they read that." Devon finally entered the room and walked to the wall mentioned in Grace's writings. "She mentioned crates along this wall. Did she write anything else of them?"

Derek lifted a second paper and read.

Whisperings carry through the thin wall from the bedroom beyond this hidden space. I do not recognize the voices, but there are three of them the first time, then silence for an hour or more, and the men return, this time only two. With Baron Whitford and Alexander dead, who would Spencer bring here? The timbre of the voices raise, and I recognize my husband's now. The other, as English as Spencer's, is unknown to my ears.

Relief wells within me that Brice is not beyond the wall. It must mean he is safe, and I pray, my son with him.

Another hour has passed since Spencer left this room. He did not find my pages. He and the other man I heard entered, though the other wore a scarf about the lower part of his face. He beckoned two others inside and they removed the crates, one by one, while Spencer stood before me to block the goings-on, but I heard them.

My husband said nothing all the while, and when the last wooden crate scraped on the board floor before it was lifted and carried out, Spencer wrapped his hand around my neck. For the

*barest moment, I expected his to be the last face my eyes rest
upon before death.*
*He released his grip and left the room. A heavy scrape makes
me think he has blocked the door. Silence followed.*

"Smuggling?" Devon mused. "Tea, wine, spirits, and more
were among the primary smuggled items during
Canterbury's time, but those make no sense with what else
we have learned from Grace's journal."

Derek fingered the edge of the paper from which he'd
just read. "She does not say what the crates held; it's unlikely
she ever learned. Smuggled exports back then included gold
and—"

"Guns." Devon mentally calculated the section of wall
next to which the crates had been all those years ago. "There
is enough room here for two crates resting side by side, the
length of which could hold long rifles. It's an assumption, but
a viable one. What is on the last page?"

Derek glanced at his brother.

"You seem reluctant to share it."

*Darkness has yet to engulf this room, so I am hopeful the hour
is not as late as it feels. Not a word from Spencer or Brice. I
write these words and contemplate how to escape. I tell myself
Brice will come. No matter what he has found, no matter what
he has encountered, he will come for me.*

"That is all, at least that can be read. The ink is faded in
some places, and the paper fragile."

"Then we still do not know what befell her."

Derek walked into the next room and returned a moment later with a book. He gathered the sheets with writing on them and tucked them gently between the pages. "I will transcribe these into her journal. Did Rhona discover anything new there?"

"The last passage is about Grace's son, believing he is not dead. The pages are blank beyond it."

"Now we know why."

"Yes," Devon said, "but why, then, did her husband not also take the pages from here?"

"He may not have had time. Again, we won't learn everything." Devon started from the room. "However, we will discover what happened to her. You have been at this game far longer than I have, Derek. What are we missing?"

They both exited the hidden room. Devon left the door ajar. It would never be used again, at least in its current form. "You are skilled in our craft as any of us has ever been. Perhaps, though, we are thinking too much of her."

Derek halted in the hallway. "She is the only spirit existing in this house, Devon. Who else are we to think of?"

"The Highlander, who we can assume is this Brice she writes of." Devon pointed to the book his brother held. "We can only draw conclusions based on her journal notes, but what does his behavior bring to mind?"

"A spy."

"Or an agent."

"Same thing."

Devon chuckled. "True enough. He would not have risked a mission, a task, for a woman."

"Unless he loved her," Derek whispered. "As you love Anne and risked all for her. The same for Tristan and Charles, and we cannot fathom how many others before us. We would each of us risk everything for the woman we love."

Devon's head tilted slightly to the side as he studied his brother. "You have formed an attachment with her."

"Do not ask me to explain." Derek tucked the book close to his chest and walked the corridor length to the grand staircase. Once back on the main level, he made for the parlor, with Devon a few steps behind.

Anne rose and held her hands out to her brother-in-law. "We have wondered where you have hidden yourself these past hours, Derek." She smiled at her husband when he entered close behind. The smile faltered when she took in the seriousness of their expressions. "What did you find?"

Derek settled onto an empty chair at a small card table and carefully removed the papers from within the book. "What I am about to read is unlikely to help us, but it is worth hearing."

CHAPTER 18

Greyson Hall, Northumberland
December 23, 1782

B rice waited for Spencer to emerge from the room into
which Grace had followed him. More minutes passed
than he had expected, and when the man reentered the
hallway, he turned a key in the lock and pocketed it.

He stood too far away to hear the words spoken between
Spencer and the younger man Brice recognized as a
footman. A clatter from the opposite corridor marked the
unexpected withdrawal of guests, who doubtless wondered
what had precipitated their host's hasty decision to see them
all gone before the grand celebration they'd all been
promised.

The two conspiring men briefly listened to the noise
before speaking again, this time in whispers. The footman
nodded and hurried off to do his lord's bidding. Brice
preferred to remain behind, do away with Lord Canterbury,

and steal Grace from the house forever, except for the silent promise she had wrested from him.

Her son must come first, for it is what she wanted. Brice called up a silent plea for her safety until he could return. He followed the footman. Twenty minutes later, he questioned his decision, for the young man led him on a circuitous route to the farthest end of the village and finally to a small farm holding beyond. At the door of the thatched cottage, the footman paused, searched his surroundings, and knocked three times before opening the portal and entering.

Brice ran behind the few outbuildings and hid behind a grain barn. When no one appeared, he crept close to the cottage and hovered near a window. A narrow gap between the two wooden shutters allowed snippets of sound to migrate toward him.

"His lordship said to do as he instructed."

"'Tis a wee bairn. He canna do w'oot his mither."

Brice recognized a fellow Scot's voice but did not know the woman behind it. At least she harbored concern for the child.

"Is the boy still here?"

When Brice did not hear a reply, he guessed she either nodded or shook his head.

"Good. His lordship said to return the boy to him tomorrow."

The woman's following words were too soft for Brice to hear.

"We all serve at the pleasure of Lord Canterbury." The footman's tone indicated it was a position he did not relish.

Brice waited for the young man to leave and waited still for the woman to move about the cottage. When he no longer heard a sound from inside, he walked to the front door, knocked three times, and entered.

The woman stood over a heavy iron pot hanging over the fire, her back to the door. "Did ye forget—"

The wooden spoon she held clattered to the floor, splashing bits of soup across the boards when she turned.

"Who are ye?"

"Who I am is no' yer concern."

Her hands trembled as she folded them into her skirt. Average in age, looks, and height, she was an unassuming woman with light-brown hair pulled tightly back and secured at her nape. She wore peasants' garments on her body and fear in her eyes.

"Yer the mon they call Highlander."

"And ye're a disgrace tae yer kind. Where is the bairn? And dinna think tae call oot. I can reach ye faster than ye can open yer mouth."

She reached for the table and used it to steady herself. "He isna here."

"Where then? From what I heard through the window, it sounded as though the bairn was still here."

"Gone."

Brice's hand curled into a fist, the temptation to strike at anything strong. "Gone where?"

"I ne'er would harm the bairn. He's safe tae be sure. Ye've me promise."

"I dinna care for yer promises, madam. Where is he?"

"Safe. I canna tell ye more, fer his sake."

Brice gave himself a moment to examine more of what she had not said. "I mean the boy no harm and am here at his mother's behest."

Her eyes narrowed then. "Ye dinna sound like a Highlander no more."

"Trust me, madam, he is still in me, and tempering centuries of our people's savagery is proving more difficult than I care to admit."

"The bairn isna here, I swear it. With me brother, he is, safe and gone. I ne'er asked me brother where he was takin' the bairn." She stood a little straighter now. "His lordship in the big house, he's no' here all the time." She tapped the side of her head. "I see the evil in him."

Brice relaxed his stance only enough to show he meant her no harm. Instinct never led him astray, but right now, it failed him. He heard truth in some of her words and deception in others. "The boy belongs with his mother. You must return him, or you and your brother will face dire consequences. I intend you no harm—so long as the boy is returned."

"I canna tell ye what I dinna ken. Me brother swore no' tae tell me or anyone where he's gone. When his lordship comes to ask of me, I mun be able tae tell him I dinna ken."

Brice swore and spun around before facing the woman again. "In which direction did they travel?"

"'Twas north, but 'twill no' be where they go. He's a wyse one me brother is."

"Not wise, madam, for he has stolen a child from its mother and left you to fall at Lord Canterbury's mercy."

The woman finally sat. "'Twas me own choice." Moisture filled her eyes. "Afore ye see me tae prison, or worse, at the mercy, as ye say, of Lord Canterbury, I mun beg ye let me speak tae his lady."

"To what end?"

"Tae tell her the bairn is safe from Lord Canterbury."

Brice leaned over the table, his face stopping inches from hers. "You, madam, are mad."

"Wait!" She bounded up from the chair. "Ye didna ask me brother's name."

Brice wrenched the door open to the winter beyond. "I am not such a fool to believe you will speak the truth, and if you do, it is unlikely your brother will use a name known to anyone. No, I will not give you the satisfaction of watching me chase a ghost."

She cowered at the vehemence in Brice's voice, and her silence told him he was right. "Let Lord Canterbury do with you what he will, for God will have no more mercy on you."

When Brice left the cottage, the sun drifted midway to the horizon, its brightness and warmth dimmed by rolling clouds. He returned on the same path to the house and rushed behind the stable when he spied Lord Canterbury racing his steed dangerously away from the building toward the village.

Whether someone had discovered Alexander's body or the next phase of Spencer's plan was underway, Brice had run out of time. He entered the house through the back entrance, ignoring a maid and hall boy, both of whom dared not question a guest of Lord Canterbury, at least until the lord told them otherwise.

Why he had not yet done so belied reason, yet Brice would accept his good fortune for however long it may last. Powerful legs carried him swiftly and with one purpose down the quiet corridor to the bedroom into which Canterbury had locked his wife. The oak-framed door did not budge at first shove. Brice grit his teeth, prayed no one was close enough to hear, and rammed his shoulder against the weakest part around the lock. The door splintered inward, nearly sending Brice forward to the floor.

His efforts gained him into an empty room. "Where has he taken you, Grace?" Faint scratches and a muffled voice kept Brice rooted to the carpet as he studied the room. When at last he focused on the direction of the noise, he walked toward it. The scratches grew louder until they resembled pounding. "Brice!"

He swore and examined the wall, finding no opening, crack, or lever. Grace's cry for him returned—from behind the wardrobe. Brice braced his upper body against the heavy oak piece and shoved until it scraped across the uncarpeted floor beneath it. A section of wall opened in the shape of a nearly seamless door, and Grace tumbled against him. Brice's arms enclosed Grace and held her against his chest. To assure himself she was unharmed, he smoothed his hands over her body until at last, they cupped her face. "He did not harm you?"

"No." Breathless, she caressed his palm with her cheek. "How did he not see you?"

"He left in haste toward the village."

Grace's eyes widened. "Alexander."

Brice nodded. "It is what I suspect as well. The body would not have been easy to find, but I was in haste, cleaning up the blood. We do not have time, Grace, for you to pack a valise. We must leave now before he returns."

"My son." She clamped his arms with incredible strength. "I will not leave without Hartley. Did you find him?"

Brice framed her face once more. "He is no longer on the estate. He could well be in Scotland now or halfway to London. I swear to you, Grace, I will find him, no matter how long I must look or how far I must go."

Grace released him and pressed a fist against her stomach. "I cannot leave him!"

"I will stay behind, but you must go now." Brice did not give her a chance to argue with him this time. He lifted her into his arms, holding her head against his shoulder while her legs hung over an arm. Only when he put her down outside the cottage behind the stable did she push against him and attempt to run off. He swung her around, his grip firm around her waist. "Do you want your husband to kill you? That is what will happen if you return now."

"My son!"

Brice held her close and kept her arms against his chest until she settled. "I swear to you I will find him."

Grace collapsed against him, her cries muffled by his shirt.

"I swear it, Grace." He inched back when her sobs settled into a shudder. "You must leave."

"*We* must leave."

"Listen to me, Grace. I have something else to finish. Once done, I will find Hartley and bring him to you."

"How will you know where I've gone?"

"Archie will take you to Scotland. My family has a home in the lowlands. You will be safe there."

Grace shook her head and shoved at Brice's chest. "Spencer will call up every man he can to kill you. It is a wonder he has not done so already."

"He did not yet know about his brother's death. Besides, I have as many men to call upon, and your husband will not want his actions known to those beyond a small circle."

She knuckled away fresh tears and bore her gaze upon him. "Does your unfinished business concern the crates Spencer hid away? Whatever they were, they are gone now."

Brice stilled before she had finished speaking. "What crates?"

"The large ones in the room where you found me. Did you not know?" Her voice held a measure of hope.

His held disappointment. "Do you still not trust me?"

"I trust you with my life, but there is something you have yet to reveal, and without knowing—"

"Damn your stubbornness." Brice shook her shoulders. "To tell you everything would be to betray the trust of my brothers. It is not my secret alone to reveal."

"You are here to stop Spencer, though?"

Brice nodded. "The crates could well be what I have searched for since coming to Greyson Hall."

"Baron Whitford, Lord Bawley, and Alexander? They are all part of this?"

"Part of Lord Canterbury's treason, yes. Your husband will soon realize the depths of my betrayal to his cause."

The door to the cottage opened, and Archie quickly entered. "All is ready."

Brice smoothed back her pale-gold locks and fiercely kissed Grace's rose-tinged mouth. "Archie will keep you safe. I've assured him you will not surprise him with a hit across the head again. There are others along the way who will protect you if need be."

Grace clasped his hand as he passed her. "Promise you will come for me. We will find Hartley together."

"I promise," he whispered before leaving.

"We must go now, my lady."

Grace stared at the door. "Are you one of the brothers he spoke of?"

Archie kept silent.

"You are sworn to the same secrecy?"

"Lives depend upon it, my lady. We are a brotherhood and have sworn secrecy to protect those in our group and those we fight for and against." As though expecting her next question, Archie added, "We have no name, and even if you press, you'll get no more from me."

Grace nodded slowly. "How far will we travel today?"

"We will be in Scotland tonight." Archie opened the door and beckoned her to follow when he found nothing amiss. "Stay close, my lady."

Once on the horses, Archie led them away from the mansion, though not north toward the border, but south. They traveled until her legs were sore, and she had no notion of where they were. Twice he silenced her when she asked a question, and finally Grace gave up. Even if she escaped him, Grace lacked conviction in her ability to survive alone —wherever they may be.

"We'll rest ahead, my lady."

Moonlight glistened on the snow, and the wind danced around them, forcing Grace to huddle deeper into her cloak. Archie unrolled a plaid, slowed his horse, and draped the wool over her shoulders. "You'll have a warm bed tonight."

She relished the thought of a fire and sustenance more substantial than the oat cakes Archie gave her earlier. Grace gaped at the two-story stone house they came upon not an hour later. Smoke twisted upward from the chimney, and candles burned in two windows. It was not a grand edifice, but even in the darkness, the idyllic setting struck a longing chord in Grace's heart. Despite her wealth and upbringing, this cottage, with its thick forest beyond, the sound of a stream gurgling nearby, and barren grass beneath the moonlight promised of brilliant growth in the spring.

"Are we in Scotland?"

"Aye. Barely across the border, but 'tis safe here. We'll be at Maclean's estate tomorrow eve."

They rode up to the front of the cottage. Uncertain if she could dismount without falling, Grace remained on the horse. "And from there?"

"That is for Brice to say."

Archie swung a leg over his mount and landed on the ground. He walked around his horse to hers, showing no sign of the exhaustion she suffered. She welcomed his assistance, and he was mindful of where he placed his hands when lifting her down. Grace wavered momentarily, then froze. Archie placed a finger over his lips, put his back to her, and drew a sharp blade from a sheath in his boot. The door eased open, and a man, several years older than Archie, stepped out. "'Tis ye Archie?"

"Aye, Fergus. You were expecting us."

"Aye. Come in now, both of ye and quick about it. Forgive me, me lady, but 'tis no' a night fer ceremony."

Archie secured his blade and held out an arm for Grace, which she accepted. They stepped into the warm cottage, and Grace basked in the sudden rush of heat that coursed over her face. A man's groans captured her notice—and Archie's.

"Who else is here, Fergus?"

By way of an answer, Fergus waved them into a narrow bedroom. In the center of the bed lay a young man with a scraggly red beard. His eyes pinched closed in pain, and sweat beaded his forehead.

"Who is he?"

"Me sister's boy." Fergus returned to his nephew's bedside. "Caught courtin' a baron's daughter and paid the price with a ball tae his chest."

Grace brushed back the hood of her cloak and draped the borrowed plaid at the foot of the bed. "What can be done for him?"

Fergus eyed her with wariness. "Nothing, my lady, though 'tis kind of ye tae show concern. 'Tis a matter of waitin' fer the fever tae leave him. Archie'll see tae ye, my lady, if ye'll forgive the poor hospitality."

Grace began to protest, but Archie's light touch on her arm stalled her mid-word. "I'll see to her, Fergus." Archie gestured for Grace to return to the hallway and closed the door behind him.

"We cannot leave the poor young man to die."

"Fergus is a doctor, my lady. Were he able to do more, he would."

Grace stared at the door for several seconds before conceding to Archie's wishes. He led her into the cottage entry. "Fergus's sister lives here, so you'll not be without a chaperone."

"His sister whose son is near to death?"

Archie nodded.

"Then she is hardly in any condition—wherever she may be—to chaperone. It hardly matters, though, under the circumstances."

"Brice won't like it, my lady."

"He will understand, given what has happened. Where is the kitchen?"

"I'll bring a tray to you, my lady. It won't be proper for me to walk you upstairs, but Brice has said you're to have his room, first at the top."

Grace studied her surroundings once more. A large stone hearth dominated half of one wall and appeared to open to the room beyond the wall. A single table and chair made up the furniture in the entry room, and three paintings, two of heather moorlands and one of a dark forest, covered the wall opposite the hearth. To her right, a staircase with a polished banister rose to the second level. For all its sparseness, the cottage exuded a cozy warmth.

"The cottage belongs to Brice?"

"It does, though others use it."

Archie did not offer up additional details, and too weary now to extract more, she relented.

"The room, top of the stairs, my lady. I'll bring a tray up."

"No. I will join you in the kitchen or at the least sit down here. And I will accept no argument."

Archie wanted to argue, indicated by the opening and closing of his mouth with no emitted sound. "Very well, my lady."

In truth, Grace was not ready to close her eyes on the day, for surely only nightmares awaited her. She followed Archie into the next room, a large sitting room, or rather a room of many uses, for it also boasted a wide oak table with a long bench on either side and a high-backed chair at each end. Several tufted chairs, each one big enough to comfortably seat a man, were positioned in front of the hearth, where a fire burned low. Archie stopped to add fuel, then motioned for her to sit at the table while he disappeared into a room beyond.

Grace sat with her cloak still draped over her shoulders. She huddled beneath it for warmth, though the room held onto little of the night's chill. A clock sat atop the fireplace mantel and showed her how wrong she had been about the time. The middle of night had bid them farewell to welcome in a new day.

"I am here now, Brice. Where are you? I pray you are safe!"

CHAPTER 19

Greyson Hall, Northumberland
December 24, 1892

Derek ignored the cold, which had seeped into the room when the fire extinguished itself. He ignored the ache in his shoulders from bending over each book and ledger he removed from the shelves to examine. Derek spared no page of any volume of his examination, and when only one shelf remained to be searched, he kept to his task.

A man possessed.

He refused yet to ask himself why.

"You'll do her no good if you don't sleep."

Derek blinked when he raised his eyes from a new page and pressed them firmly closed against the sting from having read for too long in the darkness. "What are you doing down here, Zachary?"

"I should ask you the same." Zachary entered the circle of light created by the oil lamps scattered around Derek's study and dropped a leather satchel next to the door. "It's no wonder you're alone at this hour. Everyone else under this roof is wise enough to be abed at five past the hour."

Derek stared at his brother from beneath heavy lids. "At what hour?"

In answer, Zachary pointed to the clock on the table by the door.

"I cannot see it."

Shaking his head, Zachary sat in one of the two chairs in front of the desk. "The hour is fifteen minutes past four o'clock on the early morning of Christmas Eve day."

Derek took in his brother's clothing—the same clothes he'd been wearing when they parted in the village. "You look pale or blue. I cannot quite tell. Have you just now returned?"

"Good of you to miss me, brother. As it happens, I have."

"You could have traveled to Scotland and back in the time you've been gone."

When Zachary's mouth lifted ever so slightly on one side, Derek rubbed away the sleep from his eyes and scooted forward in the chair. "Where were you, Zachary?"

"Scotland, of course." He rose, crossed to the liquor cart, and poured himself a finger of Derek's favorite whiskey. "Devilish cold out when the sun disappears." He returned to the chair, sat, and drank half the whiskey. "Are you going to ask?"

"I'd prefer to strangle you, and as there are no laws against killing fools—"

"Ah, but there are." Zachary rolled his shoulders and sighed. "Devilish cold in here, too. Did you not realize the fire had gone out?"

"No, and no one will ever find your body."

Zachary might have choked on the last sip of his drink if he hadn't already swallowed. "Glad to hear it. I'd hate to think you were slipping. Did you know there is a road from here to the border, and just across Hadrian's Wall is a charming cottage that—"

"A cottage often used by men in the agency. Yes, Zachary. I recall you availed yourself of it once before. What is your point?"

"Did you also know that since 1776, the cottage has been entailed to a Maclean family, specifically, the descendants of a Brice Maclean of Argyll. The estate also has several other properties, including an impressive manor with working farms in Douglas. From the look on your face, the name means something to you."

"She wrote of a Brice, several times." At his brother's quizzical expression, Derek explained the hidden room, the painting, and the writings left in the room. "We surmised he was the Highlander who visited Greyson Hall at Christmas of 1782, and you have all but confirmed it." Derek gawked at his brother. "How?"

"By freezing on the road to Scotland and back. I borrowed one of Devon's horses and changed mounts at the cottage, so I'll need to return for the beast after Christmas." Zachary rose once again, this time to the hearth. He added two small pieces of wood from a nearby box, a few dry spare bits of paper, struck a match, and watched it flame. He remained close to the fire.

"Agents use that cottage." Derek stood and joined his brother. "There would be no official record of an agent's name, but it's possible."

"You are not speaking in full sentences, but I follow your thoughts. You think Brice Maclean was a fellow brother-in-arms. I thought so as well. However, the agency—as we know it now—did not exist until the 1820s."

"There have always been spies, Zachary, and our agency is not the only one to never bear a name. If this Brice

Maclean was such a man, it explains why he was here. Many in England tried to use the American War of Independence to their benefit, and the smuggling scourge was often financed by men of property. It is clear from Grace's writings and Maclean's behavior that he was no friend to her husband."

"You're assuming that Lord Canterbury was such a man?"

Derek shrugged. "It's as good of a theory as any. The man is long dead, and I care nothing about what he did or why. I care only what happened to Lady Canterbury and her son; the answer may rest with Brice Maclean. A man of his wealth and land will have left records."

Zachary *tsked* and shivered when he left the fireside to retrieve his satchel. He dropped it on the chair behind the desk and resumed his vigil next to the warm hearth. "The personal papers, or what I could unearth at the cottage, of Brice Maclean. He uses one of your favorite hiding places—under a floorboard beneath the bed."

"They let you take them?"

"Only the caretaker was present—the same who was there when I slept under the roof once before. I swore on your life to return them."

Derek chuckled. "We are all too much alike. I said the same to Devon."

"Yes, but I meant it." Zachary closed his eyes and stomped his feet lightly on the carpet. "I am not cruel enough to drag the cook from her bed at this hour for a meal, and food and a warm bath, followed by several hours in bed, are all I care about now. I will leave you to your research while I avail myself of the kitchen."

Derek stopped his brother and brought him close for a quick embrace. "Thank you, Zachary."

"We all do what we must for the women our brothers love, do we not?"

"I don't—"

"That lie won't work on me. Call it love, or call it something else. This ghost—this lady—is important to you." Zachary was almost from the room when Derek called his name.

"How did you know to go to Scotland and that you'd find what you wanted when you got there?"

Zachary grinned. "A lovely barmaid in the village hails from across the border. Her father is a tenant farmer for the Maclean family. Apparently, Brice Maclean is what one might call a quiet and reluctant legend in those parts."

Derek's brow raised. "A barmaid in the village? You know how Devon feels about that."

"We talked, brother." Zachary's grin widened. "Mostly talked. Good night."

Derek lifted the flap on the satchel and withdrew a stack of papers, some more worn than others. Fifteen minutes into his dissection of each document revealed one that drew a sharp breath from his lungs. A marriage license between Brice Maclean and Grace Canterbury, dated 6 January 1783.

"Barely a fortnight after Christmas, which means Lord Canterbury was already dead. Who, then, closed the house and moved to Surrey? And what happened to your son, Grace?" Derek did not expect Grace to respond, though he hoped she lingered if that's what spirits did. In case she could hear him, he continued to speak aloud. "If you did not know what came of your son, and if your husband was already dead, then why the speculation about Lord Canterbury's move to Surrey and descent into madness or your son living with a cousin in Scotland? Who would create and spread such tales?"

Derek waited, his breath so quiet as not to be heard in the still air.

His lady did not appear.

"More fool me." Derek reread the faded license before setting it on the stack and moving to the next paper. This one set Derek's hand trembling.

Upon the death of my beloved wife, Grace Maclean, I, Brice Maclean of Argyll, make a record of my wishes if our Lord sends me to join her. A more formal record I shall make upon my return home to Douglas.

All that is not promised and entailed by right to our son, Gregory Maclean, is hereby bequeathed to Hartley Canterbury, son of Grace Maclean and the late Lord Spencer Canterbury of Northumberland, whether he be found before or after my death. I make this record of sound mind and purpose on this tenth day of July in the year of our Lord seventeen hundred and ninety-four.

"1794. A mere ten years after your son went missing. How did you die, Grace?" Derek shuffled through the remaining papers but found naught except business and land records. He hurried from the study to the parlor where Grace's portrait, for too long hidden away, hung in the center of several paintings, prominent in its placement.

"Grace, Hartley was found because his line continues to this day, though you did not find him while you still lived." Hartley Canterbury's progeny existed to this day. Derek rubbed both hands roughly over his face. "Sleep. Yes, I must sleep, or they will all think I've gone mad. Where are you, Grace?"

No amount of hope that he was closer to helping Grace could combat Derek's exhaustion. He trudged up the stairs to his room, divested his shoes and jacket on the floor, and considered the energy required to remove the rest of his clothing. He sat upon the foot of his bed to do just that, guided by a thread of moonlight sneaking between the open drapes—and nearly lost his breath.

Radiance shimmered from the crown of her pale, golden hair to the hem of a gown as luminescent as her ethereal countenance. Derek clutched a fist over his heart, where once more an ache beyond any he'd ever known pierced the beating flesh and brought him to his knees. He stumbled before he righted himself, and when moisture glistened in her eyes, the sentiment echoed in his.

A thousand thoughts flitted through his mind, yet he voiced not one. Neither of them required words, for he already knew her sorrow and he could not yet fulfill his promise to help her.

"Soon," he whispered. A tremor coursed through him, and without rational guidance from his brain, Derek reached into the void. She mirrored his action, and though no corporeal caress passed between them, she stirred the core of his soul. "Soon, my lady."

Restlessness prevented Derek from enjoying the depths of sleep, and a desire to keep his promise roused him from bed five hours after he had laid upon his pillow and dragged the linens over his naked body. A warm bath and fresh clothes revived him somewhat, and a rumbling stomach sent him to the breakfast room, where, to his annoyance, everyone was already seated and enjoying their morning meal.

Christmas Eve day. Preparations for the tenant and village party at the hall tomorrow would fill most of the day, which meant Anne would hurry every able-bodied man along to help the servants. They planned a private feast for their small group that evening, which meant Derek needed to contrive a plan between now and tomorrow.

"Derek, did you hear Anne?"

"Yes, plenty of sleep, thank you."

Charles coughed to cover a laugh, Tristan and Devon watched him with curious expressions, and all the women smiled. Anne tried again. "Zachary informed us of the latest discovery."

A faint blush reddened Derek's neck. "Sorry. Our dear brother is ever helpful. Shouldn't you still be asleep after your adventure yesterday?" he asked Zachary.

"Fit and fine, thank you. Slept like a newborn babe." Zachary smiled around a piece of toast.

Derek filled a plate with eggs, sausage, ham, and toast, and took up the seat next to Anne, across from Zachary, who received his pointed look. "Did you read any of the papers you borrowed from the Maclean cottage?"

"A few, but it was growing late and I had a long ride back, in the dark, no less. You can thank me later."

Derek tightened his grip on a fork.

"I assure you, you will derive no satisfaction from murder. And if you were to commit fratricide, I'd rather it be by a bullet than a fork."

Derek dropped the fork, stifled a retort for the sake of the women, and picked up the fork again to eat. "Not a person at this table would turn me in. Now, about the papers. Zachary's helpful visit across the border has saved me from digging a grave in the frozen earth. Our fair ghost married a Brice Maclean almost a fortnight after she reportedly went missing from her home."

"That is a wonderful piece of news," Rhona said. "Well, only wonderful if she was reunited with her son."

"And her husband would have had to be dead for the marriage to take place," Charles added.

Rhona waved that away. "An awful man, Lord Canterbury."

"Did you not say, Devon, that Lord Canterbury moved to Surrey and the son went to relations in Scotland?" Tristan asked.

Devon nodded. "Obviously someone's fabrication if Lady Canterbury married soon after leaving Greyson Hall. Was there anything else in those documents, Derek?"

"Yes." He ate a bite of ham, chewed slowly, and swallowed before adding, "Grace passed ten years later. She bore Maclean a son. From the record Brice Maclean left, she did not know what happened to her first son, Hartley, prior to her death."

A shroud of melancholy fell upon the room.

"How terrible for her." Alaina wiped away a tear. "If a child of mine . . ." Tristan covered the hand on her lap and squeezed gently. "How long did Brice Maclean live?"

"I don't know, but at least several years longer. A land record dated in 1807 bore his signature. With his wealth, there should be a record somewhere of his death." Devon glanced up at his older brother. "Devon, do you know when Hartley Canterbury supposedly surfaced in London?"

"He was nineteen, or thereabouts, which would have put him in London somewhere between 1801 to 1803. You're thinking Maclean found him after all those years?"

Derek nodded. "How else would the boy have known who he was? The Canterbury wealth was supposedly gone, yet if he was in London, he likely attended school, and he started a family."

"Yes," Anne said, "except his descendants include the women from the Gorran line . . . one of our tenant farmer's wives and Iris. If there was wealth—"

Rhona asked, "Did Iris's mother not say she descends from a third child, a daughter who was gifted Privet Farm?"

"True." Anne finished her tea and dabbed her mouth with a serviette. "A third child, especially a daughter, would not have inherited, except for possibly a dowry. Mrs. Gorran is returning today to help with the baking for tomorrow's festivities. I will ask Hatch to bring her to the parlor again."

Devon leaned over to kiss his wife's cheek before rising and pulling back her chair. "Zachary and I will see about the Christmas tree. Hatch informed me we can find some fine trees in the woodland at the eastern edge of the estate. We'll be gone a few hours, and the sun is already bright, which should speed things along."

Zachary looked down at his half-finished breakfast and back at his brother. "Ten minutes."

Devon nodded, then gestured toward Derek. When Zachary returned the nod, Devon and the others filed out.

"You saw her again."

Derek dropped the crust of his toast on the plate.

"No use in denying it, brother. You look like a man who has realized he cannot have the woman he most desires."

"It's not like that." Derek laid his serviette on the table and ignored the remaining food. "I won't deny I ache and yearn for her. She loved Maclean. I know it as certain as I know you are sitting across from me."

"Then I don't understand."

Derek laughed. "Neither do I." He rubbed his chest, then pushed back his chair to stand. "I should have told the others while they were here, but I believe all we must do to help Grace is to have her meet Iris Gorran."

"The nanny?"

"Yes, the nanny. It will take weeks to unravel the details of how Hartley Canterbury came to be found and how he lived. If we can show Grace proof that her son's line continued, she can at least rest knowing he lived a full life."

Zachary shook his head and stood to join his brother in leaving the breakfast room. "Mrs. Gorran saw the ghost, Derek, as did others in their family before her. What makes you think having her meet Iris—however that will happen— is going to work?"

Derek stopped in the massive entry. "I don't know, Zachary. It is all I can think of to do right now."

"I'm sorry." Zachary laid a hand on his brother's shoulder. "Beautiful spirits that haunt grand houses are beyond my expertise."

Derek managed a smile. "Beyond all of us, and pray we never face such a mystery again. I do not know how spirits exist, or how they even show themselves, but I have reasoned that if one is tethered to this world long past their time, then they are not privy to the goings-on of the next world."

"You have now gone well beyond my expertise." Zachary looked in every direction to make sure they were still alone. "It is no wonder others attempted seances."

"Good, you're on time." Devon walked toward them, and Hatch, with his mystical powers, appeared from nowhere with coats, gloves, and hats for Devon and Zachary. "Thank you, Hatch. Are you going to join us, Derek?"

"I will do what I can to help around here."

"Or, you can—who the devil is that?" Devon beat Hatch to the front door, walked outside while pulling on his coat, and spoke to the young rider who passed Devon a letter, then turned and left the way he'd come.

When Devon returned, he handed the envelope to Derek. "Go ahead. It's a telegram."

The younger brothers exchanged a questioning look before Derek opened the envelope and removed a full-page telegram. "This cost someone dearly."

"Patrick, though I daresay he'll send me a bill."

Derek read the first two lines before his gaze darted up to his brother. "You asked our supervisor to look into Hartley Canterbury?"

"Patrick Ashford was supervisor to me, Charles, and Tristan before you came into the fold, dear brother, and yes, I asked him. Or rather, I called in a favor. Tristan sent the telegram the day after Rhona saw our ghost."

"Quite a favor. Why didn't you tell us?" Zachary asked.

"We didn't want to give hope when there might not be any. The house is my responsibility, including all those who reside here—earthly and ghostly."

"Patrick found a record of a Hartley Canterbury who enrolled at Oxford in 1801. He married a Caroline Maclean in 1811, niece of Brice Maclean . . . Maclean had found the boy."

"You suspected he did," Devon pointed out. "Zachary, you'll want to wear your coat, not hold it. The sun is bright, but the day is still cold. Oh, and why is there a horse not belonging to us in the stables?"

"Ah, yes. I left that part out. One of your horses is at the agency cottage across the border. I'll fetch him and return the one I borrowed after the holiday."

"At least they'll care for the animal up there." Devon fit the soft wool cap over his hair and slapped his hands together. "Let us be off. The stable should have the sleigh ready, but we have a mile to cover to reach the woodland Hatch specifically mentioned."

"You've never cut a tree down," Derek prudently pointed out.

"And you have never attempted to help a ghost cross over, but here we are."

Zachary and Derek exchanged grins, and the former said, "And Anne asked you to select the tree."

Devon cleared his throat and nodded. "Can't deny her anything. Zachary, let's go. We're already late. Derek, we'll leave you to share the telegram with the others."

Before Derek could explain that there was more to Patrick's telegram, his brothers had left him alone in the entry. Derek read the rest of the message.

Brice Maclean was not one of us, as we are now, though he is known among members in the top ranks of our agency. No official record exists of his work. His wife died from injuries sustained in a fall, and he spent the following years devoted to his country and searching for Hartley Canterbury. Lord Canterbury's death remained unknown, officially, until 1786. We only know these facts because of requests for information through various networks and verbal accounts passed down through members of our agency.

My interest is now piqued and I will research further. Why do you care about a family from the previous century? Who are these people to you? I'll expect a full report in the new year.

Derek smiled when he read the last sentence, for it was the same way Patrick ended almost every communication to the agents under his purview. As Devon, Charles, and Tristan were no longer active agents, Derek would accept the obligation to inform Patrick about their off-the-books mission to, as Devon had said, "help a ghost cross over."

"Well, my lady," Derek whispered to the house, "your Highlander found your beloved son as he promised to do. Now it is my turn."

CHAPTER 20

Maclean Estate
Douglas, Scotland
December 25, 1782

S he slept with the plaid window covering open.
Moonlight poured in through the glass, though it
disturbed her not. Her chest rose with each deep breath
through her slightly open mouth. Now and then, a sigh
escaped, and she turned to her other side, tucking her knees
beneath the layers of bedding and readjusting her hands
close to her chest.

Brice guarded her from the bedroom threshold. Snow
melted off his plaid and dripped to the floor until he
unwrapped himself and laid the wool over the single chair in
the room. He paid no mind to how long he watched her,
listening to every breath, and studying every minute
movement.

A band of fearsome gallowglass warriors could not have

slowed or stopped his arrival at the cottage beyond Hadrian's Wall. Now that he was there, and rested his own eyes upon Grace, he released tension by slow degrees from his neck and shoulders until his arms felt heavy with relief.

The edge of the feather-filled mattress sank under his weight. Grace shifted and rolled over toward him, and when her face rested against his thigh, her eyes eased open and she whispered, "Brice."

"'Tis me."

The right side of the linen shift tugged down her shoulder when she raised herself to a sitting position. Her palm found a comfortable place to rest against his cheek, and her thumb traced the edge of a superficial scratch beneath his left eye.

"'Twill heal."

"What happened?"

"We will talk about it when the sun rises. We require sleep now, but I needed to see you and hear your voice." Her hand dropped to his lap, where he lifted and held it to his lips. "I will be across the hall."

"No."

She crushed her body against his. Brice lifted her from beneath the bedding, set her on his lap, and held her.

"Your heart is always so strong."

He tilted her chin up and touched gentle kisses over her brow, eyes, and cheeks before covering her mouth with his. All else fell away in the moment, and only when breathing required them to separate did Brice release her lips and helped her head find a place against his shoulder.

"What happened, Brice?"

"I would spare you it longer if you will let me."

She removed herself from his lap and knelt on the rumpled bedding. Grace dragged the top coverlet over her shoulders. "The only news I cannot endure is if—"

"Hartley lives, though where he is, I do not know."

"What do you mean?"

"Your husband hid your son away with a villager. The woman's brother took the boy."

Grace fell against the headboard. "For what purpose?"

"I suspect to keep him, but the woman was not forthcoming. It was not what your husband intended to happen. He wanted to use the boy to gain your cooperation."

"Is Hartley lost to me?"

"No." Brice framed her face and held her still as tears flowed freely. "I have vast resources, and I will use them all to find your son."

She shuddered and stared beyond him as if looking into a void. The expected sobs did not come.

"Grace?"

"Spencer did not try to stop you?"

"Grace, now—"

"Tell me!"

"He is dead."

She accepted his words without emotion. "By your hand?"

"No, though I will not speak falsely and claim I do not wish it had been me. Lord Bowley was with two other men moving the crates you spoke of. They hid them in the mausoleum."

"And found Alexander."

Brice nodded. "Yes. It is where I found them when I returned. Lord Bowley shot him with a musket from a crate fallen on its side. The two men with him ran while I focused on Bowley."

"Did he say why he killed Spencer?"

"Eventually. 'Twas a disagreement about payment. With my funds no longer available to their cause, your husband demanded more from Bowley or he would turn his name over to authorities. He will face charges of treason, anyway, and murder added to those now."

"Please, do not call Spencer my husband any longer. Any right he had to such a connection ended the moment he took my son."

"Very well." Brice smoothed a knuckle over her cheek. "It has all been too much to bear, hasn't it?"

Grace shook her head. "I can withstand any hardship as long as I know my son lives, and I have you by my side." She eased her body down until she lay flat on the mattress. Grace pulled back the bedding and held it high, until with some apprehension, Brice removed his boots and outer clothing and lay beside her. She fit perfectly against the curve of his body, her back to his chest. His arms wrapped around her torso and his head rested on the pillow with her head tucked beneath his chin.

"Did you accomplish what originally brought you to Greyson Hall?"

He didn't answer for half a minute, and then said only, "Yes."

"Will you tell me now who you are?"

Brice pulled her closer. "After we are wed."

"We need not wait for banns in Scotland."

"Nay, we do not."

Grace nudged at his fierce grip, and when he loosened his hold, she turned and rested her face two inches from his. "And we will find Hartley."

"Aye, we will find your son, and god willing, give him siblings aplenty." Brice kissed her once, holding back the frustration and passion he'd contained since first laying sight on her. "This estate is not too great a distance from England, so here we will stay until I bring Hartley home."

"Do you know the name of the man who took him?"

Brice shook his head. "His real name will be easy enough to learn. 'Tis whatever disguised name he is using—for it is unlikely he and the boy are called by their true names—that will prove more difficult to uncover. I asked at the inns between Northumberland and here, but no one remembered a man traveling alone with a boy. My search begins anew tomorrow."

"We will find him, Brice. I know we will."

"Yes, my love. We will find him."

CHAPTER 21

Greyson Hall, Northumberland
December 24, 1892

Derek surprised the women by joining them in the parlor when Mrs. Gorran was called up from the kitchen. He stayed on the outskirts of the room and offered no explanation, though he offered a hello when Anne introduced him.

He had already worked out what he believed to be the truth, but Zachary brought forth a valid question. Grace had already seen at least two of her son's progeny. Why had that not been enough?

"Master Hartley was known to be a generous man and a loving husband. My great-grandmother told us stories of him when I was a wee girl."

Derek realized then he'd not been listening and missed the question Anne had asked of Mrs. Gorran.

Anne next asked, "Is the name Brice Maclean known to you?"

"I've not heard the name before, though I know Maclean well enough. It's said we have ancestors who are Macleans, but I know naught about them." She held a finger up and tapped the air a few times. "When Hartley Canterbury and his wife—dear me, her name escapes me—bore their first child, they returned to Northumberland. My family thought he wanted to be closer to his mother and father."

Anne, Rhona, and Alaina all looked to Derek, who presently leaned against the wall next to a window. He withdrew Patrick's telegram from his jacket pocket. "Your family's history is not as simple as the stories you have been told, Mrs. Gorran." He slipped the telegram back into his pocket, for he'd already memorized its contents. "Hartley Canterbury's mother, Grace, or as you know her, Lady Canterbury of Greyson Hall, did not disappear. She married Brice Maclean in January 1893. Her son, Hartley Canterbury, went missing at Christmas 1892 and found nearly nineteen years later by Brice Maclean. Grace Canterbury, I am sorry to say, passed ten years after her marriage to Maclean."

Devon stopped long enough to take in Mrs. Gorran's wide eyes and slack jaw. "It is a good deal of detail, and I will stop now if it is too much."

The woman gave her head a slow shake in response.

"There is much we have not learned and may never learn. Brice Maclean kept much of his life a secret, or that is how it appears. He was a wealthy landowner who it seems settled money upon Hartley Canterbury. How much?" Derek shrugged. "Why Hartley returned to Northumberland? Again, we know not. It could be he wished to live close to the place of his birth. That he could gift the farm your family has worked these many generations means it was once not part of this estate, for Greyson Hall's record of ownership is verified from the time the Canterbury's lived here."

Mrs. Gorran fanned her face and murmured a hasty thank-you when Anne handed her a cup of tea.

Anne pat the woman gently on the back. "We can stop now, Mrs. Gorran."

"There is nothing more to share at this time," Derek said. "We do not even know why it took so long for Brice Maclean to locate Hartley. If your family wishes to learn more details, then I will endeavor to unearth them for you. However, it is the lady—our ghost—who requires our help."

"You think I'm to help?"

"I hope so." Derek sat in the chair next to the one Mrs. Gorran occupied and gave her the whole of his attention. "Do you remember the time you saw Lady Canterbury's ghost?"

She bobbed her head. "As if it were yesterday."

"Did she see you?"

"Well, surely . . ." Mrs. Gorran flexed her fingers and lowered her gaze to them as she considered her response. "I don't know, Mr. Clayton. She looked right at me. I thought, well, she must have seen me."

"Did you speak to her?"

This time, the rapid shake of her head preceded a verbal denial. "No one ever talked to her, leastways not that I ever heard. They tried seances as I said, but she never appeared according to family tales. You can't talk to a ghost, Mr. Clayton."

He smiled. "You'd be surprised, Mrs. Gorran. Will your daughter, Iris, be willing to help us tomorrow?"

"I'm sure she will, but it will be up to Lady Clayton to release Iris from her duties in the nursery." Mrs. Gorran's chest puffed out a little. "Right proud we are of our Iris for finding such a fine position in your household," she said to Anne.

"She has proven a marvelous nanny and well deserving of your praise." Anne stood, and Mrs. Gorran and Derek did likewise. "I will speak with Iris today, and thank-you, Mrs. Gorran, for your time once again."

"My pleasure it is, my lady." Mrs. Gorran said to Derek, "If you can help Lady Canterbury find her peace, we'll be content to let her rest. We know where we come from, and what happened during the years in between doesn't matter so much to us."

"Derek." Alaina smiled sweetly and held Rhona's hand. "Might you go to the village and fetch the doctor?"

All eyes shifted to Rhona, whose face pinched in pain. "It is nothing."

Alaina ignored Rhona. "Derek?"

He paled and for a moment wished he could take her pain into himself. When she released a low moan and started panting, he changed his mind. "The doctor's name?"

"The doctor's away from the village." Mrs. Gorran hurried to Rhona's side. "I've done some midwifery. Come now, let's get her upstairs."

"Derek." Anne waved a hand in front of him. "Will you please tell Charles Rhona needs him upstairs?"

"What? Yes, of course." Derek thought of the long staircase and fought his imagination to block an image of Rhona giving birth halfway up. "Excuse me, Mrs. Gorran." He brushed past the slight woman to reach Rhona's side. "Rhona, Charles will understand." He wrapped her arm around his neck and lifted her into his arms. Derek conjured another image, this time of a golden-haired, delicate beauty who did not have the loving and caring husband she deserved the first time she brought a child into the world.

Rhona had Charles, and both parents would love their baby in equal measure.

Swift footsteps bounded down the hallway and Charles's shout halted Derek at the base of the stairs.

"Thank God." Derek smiled at Rhona. "Sorry."

She giggled. Actually giggled. "I would feel the same way in your position."

"Rhona, it's too early!"

"The baby does not care about schedules, Charles."

Derek passed Rhona into her husband's arms. Charles held her close and murmured unintelligible words as he carried her up the staircase and down the corridor. Anne kissed her brother-in-law's cheek. "You're a dear man, Derek. Now, pour yourself a drink, then tell Devon and Zachary that our plans have changed for today."

Derek watched Alaina and Mrs. Gorran follow in Charles's wake. "What about Tristan?"

Alaina laughed before she turned down the same corridor, and Anne explained, "Tristan has been through this twice already and informed me he preferred to hang garland and berries."

"Smart man." Derek wanted to go riding, or find someone willing to face off in a boxing match, or anything other than think about what was going on upstairs. He intended to be away on assignment when Anne and Devon started their family. His brother would understand.

Morning floated into afternoon and afternoon into evening. The staff set a buffet dinner up, per Anne's request, so that they may eat when they wished. The women rarely emerged from the upstairs room, and to Derek's surprise, Charles remained by his wife's side.

Zachary returned to the village to bide his time at the local tavern. Devon and Tristan alternated between playing cards and reading, and at one point, Derek overheard them discussing an old assignment that took place in Wales.

Once Derek realized his restlessness had little to do with the mysterious workings of childbirth, he excused himself to return to his brother's study—and Grace. Her portrait drew him across the wood-paneled room the moment he entered. "Brice Maclean found your son, Grace. Did they never return to this house? Is that why you didn't know?"

"Talking to yourself?"

Derek didn't turn at Tristan's question. "It's become an affliction."

"It's all right to love her." Tristan pushed off the doorframe and approached to stand by Derek's side. "She's a beautiful woman."

"She's a ghost, Tristan. How does one love a ghost?"

"I don't suppose you expect an answer, but I'll give you one, anyway." Tristan found a match and lit the lamp next to the painting, illumination Grace's delicate visage. "Alaina wasn't the first woman I loved."

Derek faced Tristan then.

"Don't look at me like I've destroyed your image of eternal bliss. There is no one I have loved or ever could love as I do my wife, and I've told her what I'm about to tell you."

"Have you told the others?"

"God no."

Derek chuckled.

"I loved a woman who had died or loved her to a degree. She was the deceased sister of a man I was investigating. My second case as it happened, and I saw a painting of her. She was not the most beautiful woman, and I never saw or spoke to her ghost, but she is the reason I worked so hard to prove her brother's innocence, as he had been accused of her death. Everything in me wanted to protect her—her memory. It makes no sense after all this time, and yet in those weeks, I swore I loved her, and I became a better man for it." Tristan squeezed Derek's shoulder. "I never understood how much I wanted to love someone until then."

"How long after did you meet Alaina?"

Tristan's mouth curved and his entire face softened. "Many years and many assignments later. When we found each other, the years of lies, secrets, and death had hardened me. I knew, though."

Derek rubbed his chest. "So, you're saying this will pass?"

"For your sake, pray it doesn't. Not too soon, at least." Tristan slapped Derek companionably on the back. "By the way, Rhona's given birth to a baby girl."

"Holding back, old man." Derek grinned. "How are they?"

"According to Alaina, Rhona held up far better than Charles, and both mother and daughter are healthy." Tristan took another long look at Grace's portrait. "Whatever happens with Grace, you helped unearth the truth."

"Not all of it."

"Sometimes a partial truth is all we can hope to learn, and the rest remains in the past. We aren't always meant to know everything, and you'll go mad trying. Zachary has returned and Alaina said Charles will bring the baby down shortly to show her off." Tristan started for the door.

"Wait. What did they name her?"

Tristan's gaze settled on the portrait. "What else?"

Grace Rhona Blackwood inspired adoration and elicited smiles from everyone who gazed upon her cherub face. The darling girl opened her eyes a few times before deciding the comfort of one of her parent's arms and the soft blanket they wrapped her in was more interesting than anyone or anything else.

She slept while others celebrated Christmas day with an impressive display of food, from ham and fish to cheese and cakes, Mrs. Gorran's blaa buns, and an assortment of sandwiches. Tea, coffee, beer, and water filled cups and glasses. Tenant farmers and their families, along with a few villagers, mingled and laughed, and drew one of the Claytons or their guests into conversation.

Derek enjoyed their company well into the early evening. When darkness settled around Greyson Hall, and families with younger children said their farewells, adults enjoyed tea or their choice of beverage by the fire. A small group took up a game of cards, and the women sat near Rhona to catch glimpses of the baby and talk of their own tales of motherhood. Iris Gorran sat next to her mother, reprieved from her nanny duties that afternoon and evening by the housekeeper, so Iris might enjoy some of the Christmas cheer.

Derek retreated to the solarium.

He found a place near one of the floor-to-ceiling windows and leaned against the glass. Stars painted the inky-black sky with a crystalline blanket of glimmering light. The moon, with it's bright face, cast a cool glow into the dark room.

Her face appeared alongside his in the glass, and for the space of five heartbeats, Derek absorbed every facet of Grace's radiant countenance. "I wonder if you can understand me, my sweet lady. Lady Maclean, I think, suits you better than Lady Canterbury."

Her fluttering eyes were the only sign she might have heard him.

"No one seems to know why your headstone in the graveyard bears only your initials. You are no doubt buried with your husband in Scotland. Perhaps the headstone was a way to cover up that you had run away with Maclean, and all to cover up the truth of your husband's death and his treason. So many lies and rumors when the truth was so simple. It all began and ended with love."

Derek finally adjusted his stance to face her. "Brice Maclean found Hartley as he promised."

Tears charted a path from Grace's shimmering blue eyes down her fair face, to disappear into nothing, along with the lady herself.

He returned to the parlor, where candles graced the tree and illuminated the room. The guests had all since departed to leave the eight friends and family to enjoy the last of their Christmas Eve.

Anne crossed to Derek and looped her arm through his. "You saw her again."

Derek tilted his head toward her. "Is it so obvious?"

"Yes. We neglected her and you today."

Derek gestured with his head to the baby in Charles's arms. "With good reason. Tristan said sometimes a partial truth is all we learn. I thought if I could have her see and somehow meet Iris Gorran, she'd know for certain that her son had lived a good life, that he'd found love and family."

"You did not ask Iris to come down."

Derek shook his head. "I planned to, but I lacked confidence in the plan the more the idea percolated."

"What have you decided now?"

"She chose to remain in this life and this place, Anne, and only she can choose to depart it. I just don't know how to help her."

"Our ghost has held herself hostage out of fear." Anne rested a hand on her stomach. "And fear can make anyone succumb to foolish choices, even in death."

Derek smiled down at his sister-in-law. "Are you—"

Anne pressed a finger to her lips. "I only told Devon last evening. He wants to share it with everyone at once, so do not spoil it for him."

He kissed her cheek and squeezed her arm. "I love you, Anne. Devon better know how lucky he is."

She gave him a cheeky grin. "He does." Anne dragged Derek toward the others and met resistance. "You won't join us?"

"Soon." He pat her arm and released her. "I have something else to do first."

Minutes later, Derek found himself in the family's wing on the second floor. Not in the bedroom where Grace had been kept hidden all those years ago, but in the original nursery. He entered the room and shuddered when a cold draft hit his face and caused his skin to prickle. The window was secure and like Devon did before, he searched the room and found no source of the unwanted cold.

"Is this where you stay?"

Grace faded into his sight, and it took all his energy to keep from reaching out to her.

"I don't know why you chose me or Rhona to see you, and as much as I want you to stay with us—with me—you don't belong here, Grace. You belong with them, with your husband and sons." Derek shivered against the loss of her he was already experiencing. "This is where you last held your son, isn't it? Where he was when Spencer had him taken away?"

Tears sparkled in her eyes and her lips parted a hairsbreadth.

"All this time, I thought you needed to know what happened to him, but that's not it, is it?" Derek closed the distance between him and Grace's heavenly body, stopping a foot away. "I cannot speak for your son, but what I have learned of you speaks of a woman who not only loved but was loved deeply in return. Brice Maclean's actions speak to such love, and Hartley's desire to pass on a bit of this land near Greyson Hall to his child, and down through the generations, speaks of someone who never forgot his mother."

Wide-eyed now, Grace lifted a hand to her mouth where it hovered as tears fell unbidden, each one a sparkling light before it disappeared.

"All this time, you have feared Hartley may not have forgiven you." Derek did not hear her gasp, yet he imagined it all the same. He finally gave in and reached for her, his fingers grazing the edge of her subtle light. "You never failed him, Grace. Know that and be glad."

Derek swayed forward into nothing. Not even her light remained. He wrapped his long arms around his torso and walked to the window. His shaky breath fogged the glass with each puff and when he closed his eyes, moisture slipped from beneath his lashes.

When he returned a short while later to the parlor, Zachary handed him a snifter with two fingers of whiskey. "You look like you need this."

Derek sipped and let the liquid warm his belly.

"It's about time you came down. Devon insists we all be here when he tells us he's going to be a father."

Derek almost choked on the next sip. "You already know?"

Zachary pointed at everyone in the room. "Considering the people in this room, it's a wonder Devon and Anne thought they could keep it a secret."

"To be fair, she only told him last night."

"And he's been smiling like a fool ever since."

Derek nudged his brother. "Are you ready to be an uncle?"

"So long as Patrick puts me on another case during the

birth. Ah, here we go."

Devon held his wife close in front of the candlelit tree and grinned at his friends and brothers. "You have all been kind of enough to make me believe you don't already know —" Laughter filled the room and Devon gave everyone time to calm down before he continued. "A new Clayton will join us before next Christmas."

Congratulations, embraces, and kisses passed between them. When Rhona motioned Devon over and handed him baby Grace, she suggested he start practicing now. More laughter followed.

Anne slipped away from the small group and once again joined her brother-in-law. "He is going to be a wonderful father."

"He did well with us." Derek gave her a gentle hug. "You will both be the best of parents. Then again," he pointed to the other two couples in the room, "you have great examples to emulate."

"We do indeed. You will give my children cousins to grow up with, will you not?"

"Someday." *If*, he thought, *fate blessed him enough to find what Devon, Tristan, and Charles had in their brave and wondrous women.*

"I am sorry you won't see her again this year. If the legend is accurate, she will not return until next Christmas time."

Grace saved Derek from answering. Her perfect mouth turned into a soft smile, and it took Derek a minute to realize her eyes no longer reflected sadness. He watched her drift, almost appearing to vanish into one of the bright candle flames flickering on the tree. "I believe, my dear sister, that our beautiful lady Ghost of Greyson Hall will find a more desirable way to spend her Christmases from now on, with those she loves."

THANK YOU

Thank you for reading *The Ghost of Greyson Hall!*

The link below will take you on a journey to 1802 for a
bonus epilogue featuring Brice MacLean and Hartley
Canterbury.

mkmcclintock.com/greyson-hall-bonus

ENTER THE WORLD OF MK MCCLINTOCK

Welcome to MK McClintock's adventurous and romantic world, where every story ends with happy-ever-after. Immerse yourself in worlds where men embody chivalry, women are courageous in the face of unbelievable struggle, and both dare to embrace undeniable love. Escape into stories against backdrops from the majestic American West to the Victorian British Isles, with places and times between and beyond. Enjoy!

Montana Gallagher Series

A frontier family's legacy, healing old wounds, and fighting for the land they love. Joined by spouses, extended family, friends, and townspeople, the Gallaghers strive to fulfill the legacy their parents began and protect the next generation's birthright. Set in 1880s Montana.

Crooked Creek Series

Four courageous women, an untamed land, and the daring to embark on an unforgettable adventure. Set in post-Civil War Montana Territory.

British Agent Series

Three men willing to risk life and duty for honor. Three women willing to risk everything for love and family. Set in Victorian England, Scotland, and Ireland.

McKenzie Sisters Mystery Series

Rose and Cassandra are no ordinary sisters. One is scientifically inclined, lives in Denver, and rides a bicycle like her life—or a case —depends on it. The other rides trains, wields a blade, and keeps her identity as a Pinkerton "under wraps." Set in Colorado at the turn of the twentieth century.

Whitcomb Springs Series

High in a mountain valley, a place for those who have loved and lost becomes a home for those who wish to hope and dream. Set in post-Civil War Montana Territory.

A Home for Christmas

Don't miss this special stand-alone collection of heartwarming holiday novelettes set in 1800s Montana, Wyoming, and Colorado.

You may find all these and more and see what's coming next at www.mkmcclintock.com.

ABOUT THE AUTHOR

MK McClintock is an award-winning author who writes historical romantic fiction about chivalrous men and strong women who appreciate chivalry. Her stories of romance, mystery, and adventure sweep across the American West to the Victorian British Isles with places and times between and beyond.

MK enjoys a quiet life in the northern Rocky Mountains. Visit her online home at www.mkmcclintock.com, where you can learn more about her books, explore reader extras, and subscribe to receive news.

"Ms. McClintock succeeds in masterfully weaving both genres meticulously together until mystery lovers are sold on romance and romance lovers love the mystery!" — InD'tale Magazine on *Alaina Claiborne*

"MK McClintock has spun an enchanting tale deeply entrenched in the lands of Scotland and England that will leave you riveted to your chair until you turn the last page." —My Life, One Story at a Time on *Blackwood Crossing*

"*Clayton's Honor* by MK McClintock is a clean historical romance that will keep your heart beating and your palms sweating. This is definitely a novel that is going on my 'read

again' shelf! A really good and smooth read!" —*Readers'
Favorite*

"*Journey to Hawk's Peak* by MK McClintock is one of the most
gripping and thrilling western novels that anyone will ever
read. This is probably the best novel that I have yet read as a
reviewer. It clicks on all cylinders—grammar, punctuation,
plot, characterization, everything. This novel is a serious
page-turner, and for fans of western fiction, it is a must-
read." — *Readers' Favorite*

"I just finished a six-book series by MK McClintock, the
Montana Gallaghers. It is honestly the best series I have ever
read. Each person is developed into a star and given their
own book, but all the other characters are given their own
time and investment in that book. Wow! What a series. I
guarantee you won't be able to stop reading. Well done
MK!" — *Pioneer Hearts Reader*

"Ms. McClintock has a true genius when writing beauty to
touch the heart. This holiday treat is a gift any time one
needs to remember the true meaning of love!" — InD'tale
Magazine on *A Home for Christmas*

Made in the USA
Coppell, TX
21 May 2024

32547639R00109